HERO

Where are your heroes? Are they trapped inside the stories in your head, eager to burst free? Are you ready to share them, to brag of them, to tell of their deeds and battles, their daring and sacrifice? *Are you a storyteller ready to write the tales of your own heroes?*

Fantasy heroes endure. They are embedded in our cultural fabric, dwarfing other literary figures and the mere men and women of history. Achilles and Odysseus, Gilgamesh and Beowulf. King Arthur and Robin Hood, Macbeth and Sherlock Holmes, Conan and Luke Skywalker. They dominate our legends, and tower over popular culture.

The stories we tell each other begin and end with fantasy heroes, and the 21st Century is as thoroughly captivated with them as ever. From Batman to Gandalf, Harry Potter to Tyrion Lannister, the heroes of fantasy speak to—and for—whole generations.

But what makes a fantasy hero? How do the best writers create them, and bring them to life on the page? In WRITING FANTASY HEROES some of the most successful fantasy writers of our time—including Steven Erikson, Brandon Sanderson, Janet Morris, Cecelia Holland, Orson Scott Card, and Glen Cook—pull back the curtain to reveal the secrets of creating heroes that live and breathe, and steal readers' hearts.

Whether you're an aspiring writer or simply a reader who loves great fantasy and strong characters, this book is for you.

Rogue Blades Presents

WRITING FANTASY HEROES

POWERFUL ADVICE FROM THE PROS

Foreword by
STEVEN ERIKSON

Contributions by
ALEX BLEDSOE
JENNIFER BROZEK
ORSON SCOTT CARD
GLEN COOK
IAN C. ESSLEMONT
CECELIA HOLLAND
HOWARD ANDREW JONES
PAUL KEARNEY
ARI MARMELL
JANET AND CHRIS MORRIS
CAT RAMBO
BRANDON SANDERSON
C. L. WERNER

Edited by
JASON M WALTZ

Rogue Blades
ENTERTAINMENT

MILWAUKEE WI
2013

Published by
Rogue Blades Entertainment
4068 S 60th Street, Suite 401, Milwaukee, Wisconsin 53220, USA

A Rogue Blades Presents Title
Writing Fantasy Heroes: Powerful Advice from the Pros
Copyright © 2013 Rogue Blades Entertainment
ISBN: 978-0-9820536-8-3
Library of Congress Control Number: 2013932330

Cover Art: "The Hunt," by Dleoblack
Cover Design: J.M. Martin

First Edition: February 2013
Printed and Bound in The United States of America
0 9 8 7 6 5 4 3 2 1

Rogue Blades Entertainment
Putting the Hero back into Heroics!

To those who do things
Worth writing about,
Worth remembering,
Worth doing

Contents

Foreword

STEVEN ERIKSON

When asked for a single piece of advice for beginning writers, I reply with "Finish what you start." It sounds simple, and for many, even obvious. But there is more to it, because writing is a learning process, and this process is unending. I would even go so far as to suggest that most of the learning takes place in the last third of whatever it is you happen to be writing—a scene, a chapter, a novel, or a series.

There is a mindset at work here, and it needs to be approached with both humility and a kind of relentlessness. The act of creation—in the telling of a story—imposes pressure on the writer, while the purpose behind that pressure is, ultimately, grace. In other words, the reader is witness only to the finished product, and if the making of that product entailed sweat and not a little blood, well, that's between the writer and her or his maker (or muse, if you prefer; or, indeed, the face in the mirror).

When I was starting as a writer of fiction, I pored over 'how-to' books, from John Gardner to Eudora Welty, in search of secrets of the trade. Being young and inherently lazy, however, I made little effort to read between the lines. Now, years later, I have come to the belief that it is precisely *between the lines* that you will find the hard truths. They hide in the voice of the teacher, in the words they have put on the page.

Finish what you start. I voice it as a challenge, and let the silence hang. If the challenge in my tone makes the listener uncomfortable, well, *good*. It pays to be uncomfortable, especially as a writer. Uncomfortable with easy answers; uncomfortable with the process itself;

uncomfortable with sage advice. Now, that's not quite the same as skepticism, or disdain. To be made uncomfortable means that something got through, something stuck, and now you have to start worrying it. That may be irritating, distracting, whatever. And you're free to dismiss it. But if you can't get rid of it, you have no choice but to think about it.

Words of advice are freely given—the authors in this book each sat down, prepared to talk about process and the creation of heroes, and talk they have, offering up many of the hard-learned lessons they each have won in their writing careers.

But I would advise: look between the lines. These are confessions of hard work, of contemplation, of the struggle to find grace, and finally, of the distillation that comes when you finish what you start—those moments in the writing of a tale, when you can see the end, when every sentence is like skinning your knuckles, when from all the sweat and day-in-day-out grind you stumble upon realizations, glimmers of comprehension, when you find yourself in slow revelation. *That's what this was all about. I wasn't sure. I didn't know for a fact. I've been looking, tracking it down, hunting sign…and here it is.*

It's no small challenge to backtrack and see how it all fell into place: how each choice made in the telling also created *inevitability*, which now stands solid and irrefutable in the writer's mind. You only get this at the tale's end, and that is, in part, what I meant by the learning coming close to the finish.

The essays in this book are more than invitations to the cruel craft of writing fiction; they are anticipations of delivering authentic heroes: this is bared to the bone stuff, because honesty begins and ends with the writer. And nothing requires more honesty than character. No one here is spinning you a line. Each one is, in effect, saying *you need to think about all this if you want to be a writer—especially when writing heroes.*

I admit, my first time around, all those years ago, I never quite got that. But then, suddenly, I did. So, take this book here as one stone in your foundation. You'll read it, forget bits of it, remember other bits, and a few salient observations will lodge in your mind. It's not simply enough to say "Think!" It helps when someone takes you in hand and says, "Think about *this*."

As for my own contribution, I'll throw out the following:

Think about your hero. To find the hero in your tale, it pays to search inside yourself, and find some inkling of the heroic within you. Every fiction derives from a truth, but it is the act of writing that fiction that can drag you, kicking and screaming, closer to that truth. It's not a thing to be reached, not a thing to be taken hold of and known utterly. It's elusive, and even at the story's end, it hovers just beyond reach. *But damn, I got close.*

Next time I'll get even closer…

Steven Erikson
Victoria, Canada
November, 2012

The Hero in Your Blood

JANET MORRIS AND CHRIS MORRIS

The hero in your blood has always been there. Close your eyes and feel your rage, your battle, your honor, your struggle: all are part of the human condition, with us in body and mind from our earliest days. This hero is in our genes, hardwired. Heroism is our heritage: the hero in your blood will always be there.

This heroic struggle forms the basis of our earliest myths, our stories, our songs. Call it what you will. Call it species altruism, which makes a human risk life and limb to save a stranger. Call it our legacy from the Paleolithic, and before, when only willingness to risk and sacrifice ensured our survival as a race. Or call it literature's primary driver: the hero has been a focus of humanity's lore from our beginnings; wisdom from our ancient hearts transmitted at great cost—our reminder to ourselves, lest we forget who and what we are.

From the *Epic of Gilgamesh* onward, humanity memorializes its journey through story— epics of our histories and of our psyches from cave walls to clay tablets to paper to electrons. Was Gilgamesh a historical king in the 26th century BCE, who heard the tale of the Great Deluge from a survivor; who was buried in the diverted riverbed of the Euphrates as legends say? Some think so. In 2003 a German expedition claimed to have found his 'long-lost' body; yet we never lost his heroic story—it's the beginning of our own.

Fiction and nonfiction, mixing together, make myth; myth carries forward the common values which defined us once and define us still. Tales of heroes and gods, magic and monsters, upheaval and cataclysm make sense of our chaotic world, put value in tragedy, put strength in our souls. Heroic literature *is* our literature: it carries forward the best in us, makes sense of the unrest in us, and ignites the desire for greatness which inspires us.

FINDING YOUR INNER HERO

Finding your inner hero can be easy.

Simply listen. Hear the thrumming of your pulse, the urgings of your heart; they've been with you all your life. Research suggests humans organize information into story form: the heroic tale organizes our shared consciousness, our species pride, our aspirations.

Or read. Read myth, read history, read the greatest writers of fiction and the annals of the great nonfiction heroes of the ages—all of them distilled heroism for their times. Allying your inner hero with the defining mythos of humanity is perhaps the highest calling for a writer. Not through disconnected invention or by mimicry, but only by resonating with the ontology of our most ancient souls can you take your place in the great procession of the mind.

You won't find your inner hero in cartoon reductions of Good and Evil, nor in body count and mechanistic slaughter. Heroism is not a numbers game. Heroism is the triumph of quality over quantity; it has always been the exaltation of the individual.

You may find your inner hero in isolation. If so, try to render him or her whole cloth—don't reduce heroism to merely what is seen, since what motivates a hero is fervor felt and lived. To accomplish this, you must understand what makes a hero. We think a hero is someone who struggles in the service of an ideal. Our fiction reflects this, informed by history and myths from every age.

We have been writing since 1975. Since 1979, we've written heroic fantasy (or mythic fiction) about Tempus and his Sacred Band of Stepsons. Tempus is at the nadir of his career when first we meet him, solitary, beset and angry, representing heroism in its darkest form. In subsequent tales, Tempus forms an elite squadron of hand-picked heroes, mercenaries whose core is comprised of paired lovers and friends (based on the historic Sacred Band of Thebes) and the Sacred Band's ethos begins to emerge.

Our story "High Moon," from the novel *Beyond Sanctuary* (Baen, 1985), joins fantasy ethos to historical mythos through Nikodemos, one of our most heroic characters. Here Niko is badly wounded and Critias, just assuming command in Tempus' absence, comes to see him:

> *The young officer peered at him through swollen, blackened eyes, saw the bow and nodded, unlaced its case and stroked the wood recurve when Critias laid it on the bed. Half a dozen men were there when he'd knocked and entered—three pairs who'd come with Niko and his partner down to Ranke on Sacred Band business. They left, warning softly that Crit mustn't tire him—they'd just got him back.*
>
> *"He's left me the command," Crit said, though he'd thought to talk of hawkmasks and death squads and Nisibisi—a witch and one named Vis.*
>
> *"Gilgamesh sat by Enkidu seven days, until a maggot fell from his nose," said Niko harshly. It was the oldest legend the fighters shared, one from Enlil's time when Lord Storm and Enki (Lord Earth) ruled the world, and a fighter and his friend roamed far.*
>
> *Crit shrugged and ran a spread hand through feathery hair. "Enkidu was dead; you're not. Tempus has just gone ahead to prepare our way."*

Thus the connection to our heroic heritage is made, and the context of our story enlarged. Throughout the Sacred Band of Stepsons series, ethos and mythos interlace, merge with history and blend with fantasy, and each is stronger for it.

Our historical novel of the Hittite empire, *I, the Sun* (Dell Publishing, 1983), begins with a line from the actual annals of its hero: "Thus speaks Suppiluliumas, Great King, King of Hatti..." Suppiluliumas styled himself "Favorite of the Storm God, the Hero." And he was. His speech exemplifies the ancient heroic tradition that made men into emperors and changed the maps of history. His own words illuminate the novel throughout: a real hero who led his men to battle and surmounted treachery at home speaks to us across the centuries. His was an age when kings fought kings one on one—the winner he whom the gods loved best, or whose god was strong enough to prevail through the struggles of his chosen.

Such resonances among fantasy, myth, and history have been used by our greatest storytellers to evoke common values across millennia.

For example, Hesiod prays, "Come, Muse, sing to me not of things that are, or shall be, or were of old, but think of another song." Here Hesiod signals a fantasy. Blind Homer tells us that the men of his day were not as bold or brave or physically endowed as the heroes of his *Iliad,* his *Odyssey,* and claims Odysseus as his grandfather. Shakespeare and Marlowe use both historic figures and fantastical ones for their greatest works: from the downfalls of *Othello* and *Julius Caesar* to *Hamlet* and *A Midsummer Night's Dream* and *Tamburlaine the Great,* fantasies study the human condition, especially in extremis. Horatio says in *Hamlet,* of Hamlet:

> *Now cracks a noble heart. — Good night, sweet prince, And flights of angels sing thee to thy rest! —*

In between the heroes Gilgamesh and Hamlet we find humanity itself, in all its glory. Heroism to serve any fantastic purpose, if you're but brave enough to connect your work to mankind as you know it; bold enough to innovate when you do. Like Plutarch and Shakespeare and all writers from the unknown author of *Gilgamesh* onward, feel free to stretch the truth, deform history to fantasy to better tell your story. Historicity does not a hero make, but rather passion does the job.

ETHOS AND MYTHOS
IN THE MAKING OF A HERO

In *Twelfth Night,* Shakespeare's Malvolio advises, "Be not afraid of greatness: some are born great, some achieve greatness and some have greatness thrust upon them." If you equate heroism to greatness, three paths to heroism are clearly stated in those words. Modern-era writers of heroic fantasy, such as Robert E. Howard and J.R.R. Tolkien, prefer an accidental or incidental hero, even a reluctant hero: the hero as a pawn of fate.

History generally does not agree, although it will forgive the occasional sulk. History's great leaders who profess disinterest and wait to be drafted into service, demurring the while, are nonetheless statesmen or generals beforehand, and this does not occur capriciously, nor happen overnight. Pericles returns to Athens after having been ousted, and when told of wrongdoing by the state in his absence, remarks (possibly apocryphally), that Athens has the government it deserves. After the Revolutionary War, Washington is persuaded to leave his farm once more, step up to leadership—if not to "kingship"—of an America being born. This preference for the "blameless" hero is entrenched in us. We are suspicious of those who seek power. In Homer's day, the epithet "blameless" introduces a hero whose exploits are not based solely in overweening pride or lust for power.

Since ancient times, and still today, heroes must not be self-serving.

To balance heroism and historicity is to write larger-than-life archetypes believably, to write a door into legends in the making and usher the reader where your hero goes; to invoke realism and fantasy, mated, and thus put verisimilitude in the heroic heart. To do this, we must understand and invoke the heroic temperament: often capricious, sometimes demanding, but always both doing more and feeling more than others (no matter how Stoic in dialogue). To find your hero, you must set a heroic task, as the gods so often do. As Herakleitos of Ephesus says, "Greater dooms bring greater destinies."

To summon the hero in your soul you must be honest. You must question and understand this ancient model and, by doing so, surrender to its nature—and your own.

So what are the mantras, the questions, the answers that wake us to the hero in our blood? For each, this journey is unique. Some writers become the hero in life. Club-footed Lord Byron loves the ancient model so well he goes to Greece and fights the Turks beside those descended from his Homeric heroes; and dies there, of a fever, as fleshly heroes like Alexander of Macedon did before him. Later writers of heroic tales who try this method are legion, including T.E. Lawrence (Lawrence of Arabia), who retranslates Homer's *Iliad* and *Odyssey* from the Greek between his own battles. Hemingway and Conrad and others style themselves adventurers but adventurers, in and of themselves, are not necessarily heroes. Richmond Lattimore, one of the great translators of Homer, says he "lets the work translate itself." In the Second World War, Lattimore serves in the US Navy, but his translations of the *Iliad* and *Odyssey* best define his own heroic nature. Tolkien fights in World War I; his political views, his heroic sensibility, and his understanding of myth are inextricably woven into *The Lord of the Rings.*

Some writers never see battle plains in foreign lands or even the battles of the boardrooms or the schoolrooms, yet hear the hero in their blood loud and clear. Robert E. Howard never left Texas and committed suicide by gunshot; his *Conan the Cimmerian* is a compelling trip into an ancient hero's mind.

Heroism is a condition of the soul, not a raft of medals or commendations earned. Tempus says in *The Sacred Band* (Kerlak Enterprises, 2011):

> *"This was what men fought for, what men died for: a chance at life, and to fight on other days—the battle of your choice, of the body, or the heart, or the soul."*

So what makes a soul heroic? Who is this hero in your blood who can transport you in space and time and, by the honor of such company, ennoble what you do and write? How do we know him or her?

By asking how the heroic character defines itself, tests itself, grows itself. A true hero searches for redefinition of the self, and society, against a greater backdrop of humanity's worst and best.

In *The Fish, the Fighters and the Song-girl* (Perseid Publishing, 2012), Tempus asks that question, and answers it, in his terms:

> *"Then what difference does human striving make: mortal struggle, valor, pain? If you live, then live for the test of spirit, for the celebration of the heart. Live to fight on other days. Lose your beloveds one by one. And remember. Exalt the kiss of friend and horse and wind and sun, which venality cannot cheapen nor stupidity belittle."*

By then Tempus is a mature hero, and a complex one. For us to find the hero in your blood, we must at the outset define our terms for this search.

WHAT MUST OUR HERO BE?

Let us say first what a hero drawn from the literary tradition is *not:* a hero is not someone seeking suicide to satisfy inner demons, nor someone bent on martyrdom to further a political or religious agenda or end a life of misery in notoriety; a hero is not a lovesick fool or an angry youth or a misanthrope.

Heroism itself is not a fig leaf. Heroism cannot be conferred from without, nor reached by consensus; it is inherent in the nobility of a singular human spirit. Or not. The writer of heroic fiction undertakes the task of bringing such nobility to light.

Now let us say what a hero in the storytelling tradition *can* be, but may not necessarily be. A hero can be flawed (as we write ours), struggling to meet a personal standard, trying to reach goals beyond those set for him by others. A hero need not be in service to a state or nation in his heart but may be, by design or incidentally. A hero need not be a humble farm boy revealed as descended from a line of kings—but can be (if you really must). However trite that image has become, it is overused today partly because its roots are deep within our literary canon. Reading Joseph Campbell's *The Hero with a Thousand Faces* can quickly familiarize a writer with the archetypes that populate parallel myths from diverse cultures. And there are many from which to choose.

So what *must* our hero be? Brave. Determined. Tender. Observant. Honorable. Resonant. Human. In Homer, the heroes of the *Iliad* and *Odyssey* are often shown with tears pouring down their cheeks, grieving for their dead, regretting what they've lost; constantly facing annihilation, they poignantly value what they have and what they are. In the Sacred Band of Stepsons series, over the writing of its million words, we have distilled our thinking on this subject to the "Sacred Band ethos": to meet its standard (and not all of our heroes always do, because flaws are human and our heroes are human), a hero must display unflinching determination and unwavering devotion to a shared ideal and to comrades.

In *Tempus with his right-side companion Niko* (Paradise Publishing, 2011), Nikodemos observes:

> *Tempus never left a problem for another to solve. Tempus never let the pain or difficulty of an undertaking persuade him not to pursue a resolution his heart thought was right. Tempus never gave up.*

Such a hero must be loyal (although this hero can also be crafty, devious, underhanded, and resourceful, like Odysseus); must be indefatigable unto death; must be increasingly courageous, must eventually be wise. This hero must be able to admit a mistake. This hero must be a caretaker. This hero may be man, woman or child; god or demigod; sorcerer or peasant, but will always harbor a warrior heart. This hero must bring ready rage, cunning battle, acute philosophy and compelling honor to every endeavor. Sacred Banders say, "Life to you and everlasting glory." Male and female, they fight "to the death, with honor," yet this commitment is tempered by the caution of "Wanting neither too much to live nor too much to die."

In *The Sacred Band*, Sync, a plain-spoken fighter with no magic powers or deific blood, explains that ethos to two new members:

> *The dark horse-tamer, rangy and angular, leaned back against a stall wall and said, "But listen, first. You're new to this cohort. Let me tell you what it means to me. It's an honor to fight where the Riddler fights. I always know I'm on the right side. Doing more than other men can do. Sometimes you think it's more than you can do. Sometimes it is. He knows us, what we all are and what we all do. He puts us where*

*we matter. We say, 'It's better to die for
something than for nothing at all.' If you
don't believe in the commander yet,
believe in that. You'll fight battles others
only dream of, find honor and glory most
profound—not for some ruler, or town, or
city, but for all men. The Riddler says you
make the world better one battle at a time.
There is no harder life. There is no better
one, for men with a certain bent of mind
and body, heart and soul."*

A hero must be tolerant of others' beliefs, but
steadfast in his own. Here is Niko in *The Sacred Band*,
being questioned by the Theban leader, Charon, whose
squadron was recently rescued from certain death in battle
and is now among Tempus' forces:

> *"Are we hostages? Conscripts? Our
> goddess, Harmony, is she here with us?"
> Charon's craggy face worked.*
> *"You aren't hostages, not conscripts.
> Go or stay, but with all your hearts. As for
> your goddess...only you know if she is here
> with you."*
> *"Do you expect us to swear allegiance
> to your storm god? Serve him? Serve you?
> What happens if we don't?"*
> *Very carefully, Niko trod this ground.
> "My commander has been a favorite of
> one storm god or another for a very long
> time. We fighters are sworn to our
> commander, to the Stepsons, the greater
> Sacred Band, to one another, to our
> partners—not to a god or place. What we
> hold sacred is honor, justice, and glory.
> You need not swear allegiance to our
> storm god, to serve with us. Fighters are
> among us from many lands, with many*

gods and many beliefs. Believe as you will. What is between a man and his god is theirs alone to say."

So can a hero be a crusader for a nationalistic cause? Sometimes. Historical heroes nearly always were motivated by nationalism or tribalism, by expansionist intentions, or obligation to a greater whole. Leonidas and his 300 died for Spartan law. Until recent times, conquest, sack and pillage, and the annexation of land and wealth sustained armies and made war profitable. Here modern morality and ancient ethos diverge. Homer's heroes treated conquered people as plunder, took and sold slaves; humans were pansexual, loving boys and girls, women and men, as opportunity allowed. The women of Lemnos, according to legend, found their men sneaking off to Thrace to dally with Thracian women, so in one vengeful night killed all their men and lived on, man-less, until Jason and his Argonauts sailed to Lemnos in search of the Golden Fleece and mated with them. The offspring of these unions became the Minyae—the legendary race of heroes. Male and female gods and nobles favor some and doom others; equality is no part of the ancient mind. This does not make them less moral; this makes their customs different from our 21st century mores.

Can a hero be motivated by love? Often. But first define love; understand its uses by society and by the state as well as by the storyteller. Plutarch tells us that Plato of Athens envisioned, and Gorgidas of Thebes concretized, the concept of Sacred Bands—not to create an "army of lovers" for reasons of sexual politics, but to reduce desertion by setting an example of loyalty and fortitude. A warrior is less likely to throw away his shield and run before a lover or beloved.

Can a hero be motivated by revenge? In myth and early history, they often were. As Tempus says, revenge is a common driver. The Epigoni, sons of the Argive heroes who were killed in the first Theban war, attacked Thebes a second time to avenge the deaths of their fathers. The

Janet Morris and Chris Morris

15

first line of the *Epigoni* epic (possibly by Homer) says: "Now, Muses, let us begin to sing of younger men..."

Can a hero be young? Yes, although youth is not a prerequisite. A young hero must learn to transcend his inadequacies as he matures. Young Alexander (the Great) of Macedon probably had scoliosis and was small in stature; he feared never being as great as his father. This and his devotion to Homer's works inspired conquests that shaped the world. To support a deformed child in search of heroic exploits, his father Philip arguably created the Companion cavalry (having studied the Theban cavalry) to give his son an advantage: on a horse, Alexander's twisty neck and small stature were not deadly disabilities.

Can a hero be a favorite of a god or be tested by a god, be persecuted by a god, or think himself a god (as did Alexander) and still be heroic? Certainly. All of these can make him stronger. Not every hero is an Everyman. Odysseus, for one, was often aided by Athene. The relationship between god and individual is central to the heroic model, whether because of theomachy (battle among gods or between gods and humans), or because of man's struggle to understand his fate and his place in the universe. As Herakleitos says, "Character is destiny."

HONOR AND GLORY

Akhilleos (Achilles) is told by his mother Thetis that he faces a choice: he may choose honor and glory and die at Troy, so that his heroism and his name will live forever; or he can choose not to fight the Trojans and live a long, uneventful life—but history will not remember him. Akhilleos decides to sail to Troy, but while encamped on the beach argues with Spartan Agamemnon over division of plunder and slave girls. He feels that Agamemnon has purposely slighted and publicly dishonored him by giving him less than his fair share. For most of the epic he sulks by his ships and it seems that he will choose not to fight after all. But when Patroklos (his companion, cousin and lover) takes the shield and armor made for Akhilleos by the god Hephaestos into battle and is killed in his stead, Akhilleos' anger becomes overwhelming and he joins the fray. Then, as his mother predicted, he is struck in the heel (his only vulnerability) and duly dies a hero.

As Tempus says, "Sometimes a man does what he'd most like to avoid."

Randal, the unassuming warrior-mage of the Sacred Band, in his own mind more an Everyman than a hero, says this in *The Sacred Band* about honor and glory:

> *Because the Sacred Band was the best that a man could do. Try your damnedest in the face of everything. Never falter in your loyalty or betray your oath. Live and die, shoulder to shoulder, back to back. For the honor of serving by your partner's side. For the glory of dying by your partner's side. Honor and glory meant everything to these men.*

Great heroes have flaws. If a hero is perfect, invulnerable, then he is free of challenge and also free of honor. What is effortless is not honorable; difficulty wins glory and brings the hero to life. The more endowed the hero—with special weapons, special attributes, or special favors from the gods—the more daunting are the battles he must win to attain honor and glory; neither one accompanies easy victory:

> *"If the gods sent you to fight here, then the gods are fools," says Theagenes, words very soft, just a rasp that won't carry, careful not to dishearten his men, behind. "What's the price for this help? There always is one."*
>
> *"The price?" Softer still, the Riddler answers: "You'll lose all your pairs*

tomorrow, every one." He snaps his reins. The chariot horses, with Crit and Strat in tow, move closer to the Theban: one step; two; and halt.

"Then why are you here? We don't need help counting. You came to tell me this, Tempus, Riddler—whoever? What's the point?"

"The point is life. Let me spare twenty-three pairs of yours destined to die on tomorrow's battle plain and all my Sacred Band will stay and fight beside you, till the end. And I, myself. And mine. And what price there is for that, you and yours will not pay it." Tempus' head inclined to his partner, almost imperceptibly: Nikodemos, motionless, attentive beside him like a ready falcon or a hunting dog. "I've eleven pairs here of mine...and this chariot. I promise it's enough for what's in store. We'll see to all the rites, as you want them. And some will be left who remember."

(from *The Sacred Band*)

Victory, for the heroic soul, comes at a cost. A hero knows remorse in the wake of triumph, or honor of the most rarefied kind is never his:

The chapel is dim, full of the god. So many of Tempus' own ghosts are here. He bows his head and greets them one by one. Shades and revenants from years gone by crowd in, murmuring like the dead he carries in his heart. A gilded chariot gleams in the chapel's soft light: a prop for a show he disdains, in these days when it is so hard for him to keep man and god separate, distinct from one another; when so many, many wraiths come with him,

walk with him, ride with him from
battlefield to battlefield, war to war.
(from *The Sacred Band*)

Today the human race is composed of eight billion twins raised apart, squabbling among themselves for survival or fame or fortune; among so many, true honor and glory is even rarer than when our species first found its voice. Nevertheless, the hero in your blood can speak to the hero in theirs; even at its simplest, heroism and the quest for honor and glory can inspire, ennoble, enthrall— and terrify. In *The Sacred Band*, honor and glory is both deeply personal and shared among a group intent on changing destiny:

Glory wears a dreadful face today as war takes a different turn. Long spear, thunking into flesh. A youth staggers backward, impaled, whimpering. Spear pierces flesh between the nipples: mortal strike. Swords slash necks and arms. A shield-holding line drifts right, each protecting his open side. Too many open sides. Too many. Sharp phalanx just being born: an unholy advantage—new and deadly, sparking strategies so much newer and deadlier still.
The Sacred Band of Thebes, heroes all, are holding steady, each pair fielded, intentionally, with the stronger bonded to the weaker; each pair tight together while the enemy—so many, many, with gross force of numbers—overcomes their inspired battle. Sometimes, not even inspiration is enough.
Look to the souls of Your own soldiers, God, who labor in Thine awful cause. *Tempus hasn't come here to lose lives. He's come to save them.*

The Heroic Will

The essence of the hero is his will. Many people fight, some very well, but the hero is distinguished among these by his illimitable drive to overcome everything in his way. He strives to dominate reality—than which there is no higher ambition—to impose his idea of order on the chaos of the world. That this is impossible is the glory of the hero, who will not allow anything above him, who will rule all, preferably by force, even in the face of inevitable failure.

I love writing about heroes, an excuse for pure narrative, as the heroic force has to express itself in extremes of action. This that follows—a piece of my short story "The King of Norway" that appeared in the George R.R. Martin and Gardner Dozois edited *Warriors* (Tor Books, 2010)—relates the Battle of Hjorunga Bay, in the 990's, between the Jomsvikings under their leader Sigvaldi and the Tronders under Hakon of Lade, the Jarl of the Trond. The battle was part of the general century-long struggle to gather the Viking world into one great kingdom; behind it all Sweyn Forkbeard was pulling the strings, and as always, the local resistance was fanatic.

As the excerpt begins, the battle is half over. The two fleets have taken a break from bashing at each other, and Hakon has gone to look for help.

> *Conn turned his head toward Aslak. "What kind of help is Hakon looking for?"*
> *Aslak had a little skin of beer and he took a pull on it. He nodded with his head toward the island in the middle of the bay.*

Cecelia Holland

21

"You see that island? It's called the Blessed Place. There are altars there half as old as the Ash Tree. Hakon may have a problem. He switched sides once too often. I've heard his patron goddesses are still angry with him for the time he turned Christian."

He slung an arm around Conn's shoulders. "I'm glad to have you on board, boy—you're a damned good fighter."

Conn flushed; to hide this pleasure he turned, and glanced around at what remained of his crew. That took the glow away. He had not realized how many were gone. He was losing everything—his ship, the crew that made her fly. He had to win now.

He turned back to Aslak. "This Christian thing seems common enough. Even Sweyn's been prime-signed." He took the skin and drank, and leaned out to pass the skin to Raef, on the bench behind him.

Aslak was sitting on the front bench, his knees wide, and his arms bent across them. "Hakon didn't stay a Christer very long—just until he got away from Bluetooth."

"So he's betrayed everybody," Conn said.

"Oh, yes. at least once. And beaten everybody. German, Swede, Dane and Norse. At least once." With a grimace Aslak stretched one leg out and rubbed his calf. Blood squished from the top of his shoe.

Conn said, "But we are winning this one."

Aslak said, "Yes, I think so. So far."

In this narrative, Conn is in the process of becoming a real hero. One test after another confronts him; as he overcomes each challenge, his heroic persona intensifies. He's paying a high price for this; he's lost his ship and many friends, and the only justification for this is to win, and in the end, even that won't be enough.

Hakon, favored of gods, victor in a dozen fights, is a worthy enemy, somebody Conn can prove himself against. The Jomsviking captain Aslak still treats him with some condescension here, the older man talking to the primy youth, but that will change.

Writing battle scenes is fun, like being in your own video game. My trick to doing this is to choose one warrior's point of view and cleave to it, which gives you terrific focus and economy as well as maximum excitement. Show only what your man experiences, and that very harshly, and don't bother with the big picture. Instead you go for the immediate and violent, get right into the middle of the action, get him hacking and hewing.

For this legendary battle I found Google maps very useful; there are also detailed descriptions of the battle in a couple of the old sagas. The trick is to know the battle really well, work it out on paper if necessary, so I know which way to turn, where the sun is, how the land lies and where the opponents are, and then cut close to the personal and immediate and let the broad outlines arise from the detail. If you take a reader through the middle of the scene he'll fill in a lot of the edges for himself.

I had a lot of fun working on the details of how the Vikings fought ship battles. As the battle to control the North grew fierce, these big fleet engagements became more common, and the sagas described them in glorious detail.

In the blazing sun of noon Hakon's ships gathered again; the Jarl's golden dragon was in the center. They came forward

Cecelia Holland

23

again across the bay, and the Jomsvikings swung into lines to meet them.

Even as they rowed up a cold wind began to blast. Conn, pulling an oar in the front of Aslak's ship, felt the harsh slash of the air on his cheek and looked west and saw a cloud boiling up over the horizon, black and swelling like a bruise on the sky. His skin went all to gooseflesh. He knew what would happen next. This was his dream from the night before. The line of the Jomsviking ships swept on toward Hakon's fleet and the storm cloud climbed up over half the sky, heavy and dark, the wind ripping streamers from its top like hair. Under it the air flickered, thick and green.

Conn bent to his oar. Up the center of Aslak's ship came four men with spears, which they cast, but the wind flung them off like splinters. A roll of thunder boomed across the sky. Inside the towering cloud lightning glowed. The first drops fell, and then all at once sheets of rain hammered down.

Aslak was screaming the oar-chant, because of the mixed crew. Conn threw all his strength into each stroke. The rain battered on his head, his bare shoulders, streamed cold down his chest. Hakon's ships in their line loomed over them; he shipped the oar and drawing his sword wheeled toward the bow.

As he rose the wind met him so hard he had to stiffen himself against it, and then, as if the sky broke into tiny pieces and fell on him, it began to hail.

He stooped, half-blinded in the white deluge, feeling the ship under him rub another ship, and saw through the haze of flying ice the shape before him of a man with an axe. He struck. Raef was beside him, hip to hip. The axe came at him and he slashed again, blind, into the white whirling storm. Somebody screamed, somewhere. There was hail all in his beard, his hair, his eyebrows. Abruptly the booming fall stopped. The rain pattered away and the sun broke through, glaring.

He staggered back a step. The ship was full of hailstones and water; Raef, beside him, slumped down on the bench, gasping for breath. Blood streamed down his face, his shoulders. Conn wheeled to look past the bow, toward Hakon's men.

The Tronder fleet had backed off again, but they were not fleeing; they were letting Sigvaldi flee.

Conn let out a howl of rage. Off toward the west, at the end of the Jomsviking line, Sigvaldi's big dragon suddenly had broken out of line, was stroking fast away up the bay, and behind it, the other Jomsviking ships were peeling out of their formation and following.

Conn leapt up onto the gunwale of Aslak's ship, his hand on the dragon's neck, and shouted, "Run! Run, Sigvaldi, you coward! Remember your vow? The Jomsviking way, is it—I'll not run—not if I'm the last man here and he sends all the gods against me, I'll not run!"

From behind him came a howl from Aslak's ship and the ships beyond. Conn pivoted his head to see them—back there all the other men shouted, and shook their fists toward Sigvaldi, and waved their swords at Hakon. Bui in their midst bellowed like a bull, red-faced. There were ten ships, he thought. Ten left, from sixty. Aslak stood before him, and put his hand on Conn's shoulder and met his eyes.

"If it's my doom here, I'll meet it like a man. Let's show them how true Jomsvikings fight!"

Conn gripped his hand. "To the last man!"

"It will be that," Raef said, behind him.

Bui shouted, from the next dragon, "Aslak! Aslak! King of Norway! Lash the ships together!"

Aslak's head pivoted, looking toward Hakon. "He's coming."

"Hurry," Conn said.

They drew all the ships together, gunwale to gunwale, and lashed them with the rigging through the oar holes; so all the men were free to fight, and the ships formed a sort of fighting floor. The Tronder fleet was spreading out to encircle them. Conn went back into the stern of Aslak's dragon, where Finn lay, his eyes closed, still breathing, and pulled a shield across him. Then he went back up beside Raef.

Horns blew in the Tronder fleet, the sound rolling around the bay, and then the ships all at once closed on the Jomsvikings on their floating ship-island. The air darkened, the cold wind blasted. The rain began to fall, and like icy rocks the hail descended on them again. Conn could barely stand against the wind and the pelting hailstones. Through the driving white he saw a man with an axe heave up over the gunwale, another just behind, and he slashed out, and on the hail strewn floor he slipped and fell on his back. Raef strode across him. Raef slashed wildly side to side with his sword, battling two men at once, until Conn staggered up again, and cut the first axeman across the knees and dropped him.

The hail stopped. In the rain they battered at a wall of axe blades trying to hack their way over the gunwale. Horns blew. The Tronders were falling back again. Conn stepped back, breathing hard, his hair in his eyes; his knee was swelling and hurt as if somebody was driving a knife into it. The sun came out again, blazing bright.

On the next ship Bui swayed back and forth, covered with blood. Both hands were gone. His face was hacked to the bone. He stooped, and looped his stumped arms through the handles of his chest of gold.

"All Bui's men overboard," he shouted, and leapt into the bay, the gold in his arms. He sank at once into the deep.

As the battle turns against him, Conn's will rises in defiance. He cannot give up, it just isn't in him, and when he sees Sigvaldi fleeing, his reaction isn't dismay but scorn and contempt. This is the hero in him, which will not tolerate defeat. From battling other men, now he is battling the gods themselves, and never backing down.

Bui fails the test of heroism, in a sense, choosing to drown himself rather than fight on, although one wonders how somebody fights with both hands missing. All this is of course straight out of the old saga. Bui allegedly turned into a dragon, sitting over his hoard of gold.

Meanwhile, surrounded and hopelessly outnumbered, Conn and the others defend against Hakon's methodical assault.

Cecelia Holland

27

The sunlight slanted in under a roof of cloud. The long sundown had begun. Beneath the clouds the air was already turning dark. Hakon's horns blew their long booming notes, pulling his fleet off.

Aslak sank down on a bench. The side of his face was mashed so that one eye was almost invisible. Raef sat next to him, slack with fatigue. Conn went down the ship, whose whole side had taken the Tronder attack. He was afraid if he sat down his knee would stiffen entirely. What he saw clenched his belly to a knot.

Arn lay dead on the floor, his head split to the red mush of his brain. The two men next to him were bleeding, but alive, were Jomsvikings, not his. Beyond them Rugr slumped, and Conn stooped beside him and tried to rouse him but he fell over, lifeless. Two other dead men lay on the floor of the ship and he had to climb across a bench to get around them. He went up to the stern, where Finn lay, still breathing, in the dark.

Conn laid one hand on him, as if he could hold the life in him. He looked back along the ship, at the living and wounded, and saw no other face that had rowed on Seabird with him save Raef's. Along the length of Aslak's ship, he met Raef's eyes, and knew his cousin was thinking this too.

The ship-fortress was sinking. All over the cluster of lashed hulls, men were dipping and rising, bailing out the water and ice. Several other men came walking across the wooden island, stepping from gunwale to gunwale. They were gathering down by Aslak and Conn went back that *way, wading through a soup of hail and rainwater that got deeper toward the bow. He sat down next to Raef, with the other men, slumped wearily around Aslak.*

All save him and Raef were Jomsvikings. Havard had a skin of beer and held it out to Conn as he sat. Beside him another captain was looking around them. "How many of us are left?"

Aslak shrugged. "Maybe fifty. Half wounded. Some really bad wounded." His voice was a little thick from the mess of his face.

Conn took a deep pull on the skin of beer. The drink hit his stomach like a fist. But a moment later the warmth spread through him. He handed the skin on to Raef, just behind him.

The Jomsviking across from Conn said, "Hakon will sit out the night on the shore, in comfort. Then they'll finish us off tomorrow, unless we all just drown tonight."

Conn said, "We have to swim for it." He had a vague idea of reaching shore, and walking around and surprising Hakon from behind.

Havard leaned forward, his bloody hands in front of him. "That's a good idea. We could probably make that side, there." He pointed the other way from Hakon.

"That's far," Raef said. "Some of these men can't swim two strokes."

Aslak said, "We could lash some spars together. Make a raft."

Havard leaned closer to Conn, his voice sinking. "Look. The ones who can make it, should. Leave the rest behind— they're dying anyway."

Conn thought of Finn, and the red rage drive to his feet. He hit Havard in the face as hard as he could. The Jomsviking pitched backward head over heels into the half foot of water on the floor. Conn wheeled toward the others.

"We take everybody. All, or none."

Aslak was grinning at him. The other men shifted a little, glaring down at Havard, who sat up.

"Look. I was just—"

"Shut up," Aslak said. "Let's get moving. This ship is sinking."

It's in the nature of the hero to seek out the greatest challenge, to try himself against the ultimate adversary. Staring defeat in the face Conn refuses to submit, and now he stands defiant of death itself. The situation is hopeless, but he will not yield, and the Jomsvikings are all a little awed at his passionate courage. They make a raft and try to escape.

In the slow-gathering dark they tied spars together into a square, and bound sails over it. The rain held off. On the raft they laid the ten wounded men who could not move by themselves, and the other men swam behind the raft to push it.

The icy water gripped them. They left the sinking ships behind them. At first they moved steadily along but after a while men started to lag behind, to drag on the raft. Havard cried, "Keep up!" Across the way someone tried to climb onto the spars and the men beside him pulled him back.

Next to Conn, Aslak said, "We'll never make it." He was gasping; he laid his head down on the spar a moment. Conn knew it was true. He was exhausted, he could barely kick his legs. Aslak lost his grip, and Conn reached out and grabbed hold of him until the Jomsviking could get his hands back to the spar.

Raef said, breathless, "There's a skerry—"

"Go," Conn said.

The skerry was only a bare rock rising just above the surface of the bay. They hauled and kicked and dragged the raft into the low waves lapping it. The rock was slippery and it took all Conn's strength to haul Finn up off the raft. Raef dragged Aslak after them and above the waterline they lay down on the rock, and instantly Conn was asleep.

Hail fell again in the night. Conn woke, and crawled over to Finn, to protect him from the worst of it. After the brief crash abruptly stopped he realized that the body under him was as cold as the rock.

He thought of the other dead—of pop-eyed Gorm, and Odd, whose sister he had loved once, and Skeggi and Bjorn, Sigurd and Rugr—he remembered how only the night before, they were all alive, speaking of the battle to come, how its fame and theirs would ring around the world until the end of time—now who would even remember their names, when all those who knew them were dead with them? The battle might be a long-told story but the men were already forgotten.

He would remember. But he would be dead soon himself. Hakon had beaten him. He put his face against the cold stone and shut his eyes.

In many ways the hero is in love with death, the final challenge, the battle nobody wins. The hero's life is a search for the great, defining fight, the clash that will prove him at last to be one over all, and death is the only worthy adversary. In his struggles he often deals death around him, so he's both death's opponent, and death's ambassador. He is familiar and comfortable with death. It's living on after failure he cannot abide, defeat and submission he cannot tolerate.

And of course Hakon has not beaten Conn here. If you want to know how it comes out, read the story, and my novel *Varanger* (Forge Books, 2010) that follows Conn and Raef into Russia and south to the Black Sea, to do battle with the Byzantines themselves.

Taking a Stab
at Writing Sword and
Sorcery

IAN C. ESSLEMONT
co-creator of the world of Malaz

Let's face it: we writers of the fantastic (heroic sword and sorcery in particular) face the extraordinarily difficult task of establishing an entire new world for the reader. How to convey all the teeming details and information we have in mind? The temptation to jam in everything can be overwhelming. My purpose here is to argue against this 'telling' impulse.

As a fellow writer and participant in various writing workshops, one of the most common traps I see in the writing of our genre, aspiring and veteran, is this irresistible urge to stuff one's story with all the amassed background particulars of one's world-building plans. All this history, geography, philosophy, and politics is of course what we call 'exposition,' or expository, prose. Simply put, it is the direct telling of information to the reader. More or less contrasting to this category of prose is what is called 'dramatizing.' Dramatization refers to all the work put into creating an actual physical scene for the reader to inhabit where the story, the drama, is enacted. Creating this dream experience of inhabiting another world is of course our main goal as fantasists, but relying too much on exposition ('telling' information), rather than dramatization ('showing' scenes), is not the way to achieve it. This is true for all writing but is especially important for heroic fantasy where visceral 'bloody'

Ian C. Esslemont

33

sensual evocation and participation is of course one main goal.

If in feedback on your drafts and writing efforts to date you have ever been told the old saw 'Show, don't tell,' then you have run afoul of our subject at hand. This maxim is the pithy warning to avoid exposition in favor of dramatization, and it can apply to the big picture of story and narrative as well as to sentence and word level usage as well. Let's take a look at each of these two major levels of concern.

EXPOSITION, or *Too Much Information!*

Congratulations! Now that you have spent seven years exhaustively researching and building your world it is time to face the hard truth that none of those shelves of information belong in your fiction. So difficult to swallow is this truth that beginning writers often refuse to accept it and insist upon dropping in enormous blocks of description or mini-essays of world history.

None of this belongs in the fiction. These expository passages, sentences, or paragraphs are abysses that suck up all of your hard-won forward impetus; they stagnate momentum; they kill the reader's dream of participation. They...well, you get the idea. These are among the most deadly of the pits out there lurking for the aspiring heroic fantasy genre writer.

This temptation to slip in the explanatory background details is understandable. But resist. Details, yes. But salient and revealing details only. What are sometimes called 'telling details.' Meaning ones that are 'telling' (in the revealing sense) of the character or world.

In the interests of demonstration I will provide a few written examples. Normally I would never use my own work to demonstrate any issue, but in the spirit of the classic egalitarian workshop setting I will supply 'case-study' rough work. And let me reiterate: these are not presented as some sort of gems of elegant prose. Far from it. These are rough sketches meant to demonstrate that writing—good writing—is all about revision and re-visioning.

The first test case is an example of a possible opening. Now, as discussed above, openings are notoriously difficult. Especially so for the fantasist attempting to establish a new world or setting. The temptation to pack in those expository clauses, sentences, or blocks of background can be almost impossible to resist—but you must. In the case of openings less is very often more.

And just what is meant by this 'less is more' cliché anyway? Well, let's say for the purposes of this example that I want to begin a heroic fantasy piece that happens to be historical. Robert E. Howard wrote a lot of what can be called historical heroic tales. The Solomon Kane novels come to mind, as do his many westerns and tales of the oil-boom days of the southwest. So I see no problem with historical heroic fantasy. And let's open the tale by telling *everything*. Complete exposition.

> *Sometime in the late tenth century a ship sank in a storm off the south coast of Sicily. It carried a noble Norman lady escorted by a band of knights. Scavengers looted a horse and some personal possessions from the wreckage. The only survivor, one of the lady's bodyguard, later reclaimed the property.*

You might notice that expository telling is a *lot* easier than showing—that is, dramatizing. Dramatizing requires the actual building of a scene, giving details of geography, weather, landscape, and of course character. All this takes up a great deal more space than just *telling* the reader what you want them to know. And is a lot harder work. But before going on into everything else this piece of exposition lacks let's compare it to an opening where far *less* is directly 'told' to the reader:

Ian C. Esslemont

35

That night the boom of sails and the crash of timber sounded through the storm alerting the villagers that their coast had claimed yet another ship. The men who set out braving the rain and driving winds first came across a horse all alone on the shore. It was wary but exhausted, and between the five of them they managed to catch hold of its bridle. They looted the washed-up corpses of two unfortunates then searched among the rest of the debris. A chest of waterlogged cloth yielded a pouch containing a rich trove of a lady's personal jewelry; a keg bobbing among rocks proved half-full of wine. Of rope and timber there lay plenty, but such mundane wave-wrack they spurned. Eventually, the chilling spray drove them from the shore. They collected their gleanings in bags and knotted cloths and headed back to the village.

In the largest stable the men tied up the horse then started a fire to sit and sort through the goods. They threw plenty of wood on the blaze as they were cold and wet through. They ate salted pork one had discovered. The wine went down in many toasts to their dead benefactors.

Perhaps it was the roaring fire and the numerous toasts, but none noticed things were awry until one turned to see the horse untied and a stranger standing next to it. He was tall, in a torn sodden shirt and trousers. His hair was lighter than their curly black, and he was fair where sun and wind hadn't burnished him as dark as they.

"Any of you speak Frank?" he asked into the long silence.

The five edged back from the fire. Hands went to belts where bone and wood handled knives rested. One glanced to his companions then back to the newcomer, his eyes gleaming in the firelight. He answered in kind. "Yes. A little. Why? You are Frank?" The five spread out surrounding the man.

"No," the newcomer answered. "Norman." He rested a hand on the horse's neck. "And the owner of this horse."

The spokesman held out his arms, advancing. "A bold claim. And wrong. The horse is ours. We found it."

The Norman's mouth tightened in disappointment. He twisted a fist in the horse's long mane. "Don't make me prove it," he said with something almost like regret.

The spokesman laughed, waving to his companions. "Some beggar shuffles into Pozzallo and claims our possessions!" The others answered his laughter. Two moved to block the open doors where the wind-whipped rain still slashed the night. "Prove it, then," this one taunted.

The man edged his head aside in obvious reluctance. "Just hand over everything you picked up and I'll be on my way."

"No. You walk away...now," and the spokesman drew his belt knife, crouching.

The newcomer shouted something in another language and the horse lunged forward, its head darting down, teeth flashing. The spokesman recoiled, howling and shrieking. He staggered, blood gushing from the red ruin that was his face

Ian C. Esslemont

to crash into a post and fall writhing in agony. His companions rushed in but the horse reared, forelimbs lashing, and they scrambled away to disappear into the rain and darkness.

Ignoring the whimpering bloodied thing in the dirt, the man gathered up what looted possessions he could find. Then, knotting his fist once more through the horse's long mane, walked it out into the night.

Now, this second version of the opening 'tells' far less directly to the reader of the exact world setting, the historical period, the circumstances. Yet it is much longer. This is because 'showing' demands that one create an actual scene (a *place* that the characters and readers slip into and truly occupy). Yet, in the creation of a scene, it actually tells the readers so much *more* about the world.

At this point things get a little tricky. The dramatized opening does of course tell an active engaged reader a fair bit. But it does this *indirectly*, by showing. Now some of you may be *tisking* at me right now having noted that I did cheat a little by telling a few salient facts in the dialogue (strictly speaking a no-no). Ideally, one mustn't warp dialogue into being just another tool to force information onto the reader—if you do, and the resultant dialogue reads forced or out of place, then change it. In the above example I leave it to the reader to decide whether this is the case or not.

DRAMA, or *Action!*

Another major problem with any block of exposition is that it lacks something vital to heroic fiction—it lacks action and drama. There's no excitement in the spoon-serving of information. The reader doesn't have to *discover,* or participate, in anything. And so the storytelling lies flat and uninteresting.

Yet of course there remain untold ways our opening sketch can still be improved. For one thing, reading is very much a matter of taste and so some might argue that in fact *more* explanation is needed here. Fair enough. The scene may be rewritten to have the scavengers come across the drowned corpse of the noble lady herself, a fine sword, or a far greater trove of riches. A wealth of options exists; so long as all involve further action and dramatizing…

In any case, the reader now has work to do. Puzzles to solve. A canvas to fill. This is exactly what we writers want—we want the reader to have to work for every scrap of information. In this manner they will feel involved in the 'dream' and will participate as the active partner the writer needs.

For a further fine-tuning of how to avoid expositional telling in preference to showing through *dramatizing*, let us consider another more focused example. Here, our point of view protagonist is in the world of Malaz and is journeying for the first time to a large metropolitan center named Li Heng:

All through the final day of Toven's approach up the trader road, the walls of Li Heng reared against the surrounding Seti plain like a distant butte or cliff outcropping. In fields, grain and market garden plots looked ready for harvest. Locals pulled carts burdened with produce while sheep and hogs jostled him on their way to be butchered.

Many of the fields also boasted curious stone mounds that mystified him. After noting a few of these great piles he overtook a girl carrying an awkward yoke suspending baskets of manure.

Ian C. Esslemont

"Those heaps of stones," he asked.
"What are they?" The girl flinched to be
addressed by a stranger and peered up at
him, terrified.
"The stones ...?" he repeated.
"You must be joking," the girl snorted
and peered about nervously.
"No," he answered, rather irritated.
"How could anyone alive not know
such a thing as that?" she said in open
amazement.
Toven bit back on his anger and
offered, quite dryly: "Someone not from
around here." Closer now he wrinkled his
nose at the stink. The cow shit, one must
hope.
The girl laughed now openly mocking.
"Not gonna last too long around here if
you don't know the simplest thing such as
that!"
"Look child," Toven snapped before
managing to get the better of his temper,
"How can I know these things—if you
keep prattling on without telling me*!"*

Let's examine this scene by looking at word-level
cases of our 'telling' transgression. For example, the
image (or rather, the lack of one): *In fields, grain and
market garden plots looked ready for harvest.* Here,
again, we are simply told something without being shown
what any of it actually looks like. But more to the point
the true failure here, or in truth the *missed opportunity*, is
the vague abstract language. This is the greater underlying
danger of telling using adjectives and exposition. Abstract
language fails to create concrete sensual details that can
be touched, seen, or heard in the mind of the reader. For
an aspiring writer of sensual, involving heroic fantasy,
this is the far worse trap hidden behind reaching for an

adjective to describe something. Abstract language is almost useless and must be avoided at all costs.

Let's see below how concrete descriptive language can *show* the fields ready for harvest. Also, further down we come to the abstract term 'awkward.' It is an adjective modifying the burden of the yoke. It too represents an opportunity. Let's *show* that awkwardness of the yoke's burden.

All through the final day of his approach up the trader road, the walls of Li Heng reared against the surrounding Seti plain like a distant butte or cliff outcropping. In fields the heavy heads of grain bowed and nodded in the wind, while in market garden plots gourds and melons fattened under the sun. On the road locals crowded him as they pulled carts heaped with produce, and sheep and hogs jostled him on their way to be butchered.

Many of the fields boasted curious stone mounds that mystified him. After noting a few of these great piles he overtook a girl shuffling stiff-legged beneath a six-foot pole slung across her shoulders. Two baskets hung from the yoke, each over-brimming with manure. The burden had scraped her bare shoulders raw and bloodied.

"Those heaps of stones," he asked. "What are they?" The girl flinched to be addressed by a stranger and peered up at him, terrified.

"The stones ...?" he repeated.

"You must be joking," the girl snorted and peered about nervously.

Everyone might have noted that even *more* adjectives clutter this—rather over-heated—revision. However, at

least these are evocative ones tied to sensual details all of
which add up to physical images that can be seen and felt
by the reader. I also beefed up the description of the road
by showing how it is more 'crowded.' Now, after being
scolded for adjective use it is understandable that the
aspiring writer may come to believe that *any* adjective is
one too many. The truth is this is not the case. Adjectives
and adverbs have their place in prose; they appear in all
writing from the high to the low. The knack is not to rely
overly much on them. Consider the goal of restricting
their use as a Platonic ideal for which to constantly strive.
Look back over your prose and you may find that each
usage is actually an opportunity for dramatization just
waiting to be explored. I can almost guarantee that your
work will come out all the stronger from exploiting these
passed-over chances to broaden and deepen the heroic
sensual experience for the reader.

Further along in the draft a sharp-eyed reader might
have spotted yet another possibility for revision: *The girl
flinched to be addressed by a stranger and peered up at
him, terrified.* Terrified? How so? What does that mean?
What does her fear *look* like? Yet another opportunity to
wrench one's abstract language back down to the concrete
of flesh and blood. Something about the girl's eyes and
facial expression, I should think. And so on.

Also in this brief scene readers may have noted how I
played with reader's expectations (or perhaps fears) of
'telling' and the transmission of information. Normally,
such an encounter might be used for that stereotypical
expositional dump of background information about the
city, its environs, and history. Yet it is incumbent upon
any writer to try to place oneself into the point of view of
each character. So, consider this poor girl: struggling
beneath her load, in pain, no doubt hungry, why should
she oblige some callow young fellow who has the
insensitivity to quiz her while she can hardly walk? I
know I wouldn't be in a good mood if I were in her
position. Therefore, in this case, it would perhaps be too

convenient for her to come forth with all the information our lad, and the reader, might need to know.

The above encounter, then, is something of a demonstration of how, in many cases, it is the *withholding* of information and not its easy handing over that creates tension and dynamism in any scene—that all important *drama* in dramatization—certainly necessary for a heroic story. This quality is that other vital aspect of writing that exposition, telling verses showing, weakens.

On a final note, I chose to tackle this particular aspect of writing because it is all too salient to my own prose efforts. We who follow the path of writing must keep in mind that it is an on-going journey of discovery and refinement. One never 'arrives.' We are all apprentices striving to improve our craft. The lessons here are ones I must constantly keep in mind as well. By way of encouragement I suggest you trust in our active fantasy readers who are among the best out there in their willingness to give you a chance. They want you to succeed because they want that dream—just as much as you hope to achieve it.

Writing Cinematic Fight Scenes

BRANDON SANDERSON

Jim exploded through the doors to the hideout. Thugs stood; yells were like thunder. Jim flew into battle, a storm of fists and anger. Jim punched one of the thugs. The thug's fist blocked. Jim punched again. The thug blocked again. Jim was a fury, a woodsman chopping at wood. He knocked that thug down with a punch. Another thug kicked. And Jim blocked. And Jim kicked that thug. And the thug fell down. And...

And I challenge you to write a paragraph duller than that one. (Okay, so you can probably do so if you try hard enough. Please, don't.)

If you're going to write about great heroes, chances are good that you're going to need to write great fight scenes. Fight scenes in books, however, fascinate me—particularly because it's so easy for them to turn out to be horribly, mind-numbingly, night-at-an-awards-showingly **BORING**. Of course, pretty much any kind of scene—comedy, action, or drama—can turn out boring when written by the inexperienced. Fight scenes are special in that many newer writers try so hard to be exciting with

Brandon Sanderson

45

them, only to succeed in making them more tedious for their efforts.

Heroic genres, in particular, tend to live or die on their fight sequences. So, I figure one of the best ways to teach someone to write this kind of fiction is to talk about ways I've found to avoid dull action sequences. It's only one man's experience, and like all writing advice, it should be tested cautiously and discarded if it doesn't work for you. What helps one author doesn't always help another.

Hopefully, however, you can find something in here to help keep your action sequences from turning into the most skippable sections of your story.

THE DREADED BLOW-BY-BLOW

The paragraph I wrote at the start of this article is exaggeratedly bad. Unfortunately, I often read sequences that aren't much better. It seems that new writers instinctively write action sequences as dry lists of "who hit whom" and "who missed whom" exchanges.

One reason for this might have to do with the prevalence of visual storytelling mediums. Television, video games, and films—particularly those with highly choreographed fight sequences—have changed the way we view action sequences and heroic fight scenes. Much blow-by-blow writing I read seems to have been directly influenced by great fight sequences from action cinema.

The thing is, blow-by-blow fighting can work wonderfully in visual mediums. If you haven't seen it before, do an internet search for the "ladder scene" from Jackie Chan's film *First Strike*. Through use of absolutely stunning fight choreography, Jackie can go for an extended period kicking, dodging, and punching without it feeling boring. A different example of this would be the single-shot fight sequence from Tony Jaa's *The Protector*. Both of these use environment, cinematography, and choreography to create a low-dialogue sequence that is absolutely captivating.

Unfortunately, the same thing—even dressed up—often becomes excruciatingly dull in fiction. There are some writers who do blow-by-blow well, but it requires a very specific type of story, and is best in short bursts. So my first bit of advice for authors is simple: remember that you're writing a book, not a film.

The two storytelling mediums tickle different nerves and use different types of visualization. Books are never going to be able to compete with films when it comes to quick blitz action sequence for in books, the *reader* must supply much of the work done by the cinematographer in film.

As powerful as the imagination is, this requires effort—and a few missteps in the writing can result in a lost reader. In addition, the imagination needs good priming to encourage it to expand and supply properly powerful sequences. If you don't lay your groundwork correctly, the reader isn't going to do his or her part supplying exciting visuals, and you'll end up with a terrible scene.

I've got three specific suggestions to help you fix these sorts of narratives, and will apply each one in turn to the paragraph I wrote at the start, transforming it (hopefully) from a dull blow-by-blow to a dynamic sequence with a focus on a single, engaging hero standing off against a crowd of villains.

PRINCIPLE ONE: CLARITY FIRST

Clarity as a rule is important for good fiction in any form, but I feel it's specifically important for fight sequences. As I said above, if you lose the reader, your scene will become an unredeemable disaster. For this conversation, I see clarity in action sequences as having two main parts:

✦ First, accurately and solidly setting up a scene before you begin the action.

✦ Second, maintaining the reader's focus on the hero and clearly showing where people are moving in relationship to one another.

Setup is probably the more important of these two. If your reader doesn't have a good handle on the layout of a scene, you'll fail before you start. In fact, if you set things up properly—drawing the reader into the scene at the start—they'll often keep with you even if you make mistakes later on. When you set a scene, let us know ahead of time how many people there are, their general relationship to one another, and their spatial relationship to the environment.

This probably sounds obvious to you, but I can all but guarantee you're doing a worse job of it than you assume. Setup is king in these kinds of sequences, and if you've never taken time to specifically think about how to lay things out—and how to describe that layout in the most clear way possible—I suggest you do so.

The second half of this conversation has to do with blocking, which is a stage term for the motions characters make—where they are going and what they are doing. Without clear blocking, a fight sequence can quickly devolve into a muddy blur of some people (maybe) getting hurt, and others (maybe) escaping. This is dangerous for you, as when you are writing specifically heroic fiction, you're going to work hard to suspend disbelief. You *need* to encourage your reader to visualize an action sequence to be able to view your hero as being in danger—if not, they will simply fall back into the assumption that your hero cannot lose, and will skip the fight to get on to the next portion of the story.

This isn't to say that every single moment in the scene should be described. What you need is enough information to give a feel for where everyone is and for the mood and layout of a scene, but not so much information that the story drags. Getting that balance right takes practice. As we'll speak of later, often a few small details are all you need—but make those details vivid.

I've found that it's particularly helpful to keep abstract language to a minimum in fight sequences. The sentence I wrote above—"Jim flew into battle, a storm of fists and anger."—is the type that many new writers find evocative. However, it's basically a series of abstract metaphors that serve to confuse the reader and keep them from really visualizing what is happening.

Try to keep your language neat, crisp, and specific. Minimize metaphors, particularly when establishing your scene. Here is a quick retooling of the sequence above, where I have begun to clean things up and do some proper set up.

> *Jim burst through the doors to the hideout, slamming them open to either side. A group of thugs sat at the center of the narrow, dim chamber. It had once been a kitchen, with doors at either end, counters along the walls. The thugs at the table stood up, throwing back chairs, exclaiming in surprise.*
>
> *Two thugs stood just inside the doors, standing guard. Jim ignored the six at the table for now, attacking the two nearby. He took the first down with a kick to the chest, then spun on the second, blocking a punch with his forearm. Jim pushed in close and threw a shoulder into the man's chest, crushing him back against the wall beside the doorway.*

This is a big step in the right direction. It's still bland, but at least we know how many people we're fighting and generally where they are. The more we do things like this, the more our hero—and the danger he is facing—will become real to the reader.

PRINCIPLE TWO: IMMERSION

For all of film's strengths—and they are many—I believe that prose can be more immersive. We can draw a reader in to a scene and make them really *feel* what it's like to be the characters.

Part of establishing a scene should include an effort to take the reader and stuff them into the hero's shoes. Replace the abstract, metaphoric language with character passions, goals, and motivations. Fill out your descriptions with increased use of high-sensory language.

Don't just tell us what the setting looks like, let us feel the humidity, hear the wheezing of the smoker's cough, smell the pungency of a beggar's breath. Including a few lines of powerfully concrete description at the start of a scene can go a long way toward solidifying a reader's focus.

I'd argue that this is even more important for action sequences than dramatic ones. If you're writing a contemplative inner monologue for a woman walking home from a wretched date, her thoughts and concerns can be the focus. However, if you're writing a heroic fight sequence, you will depend on the reader specifically imagining the proper terrain and blocking. Giving them an evocative sensory experience can coax the proper imaginings. In a way, your "special effects" as a writer are directly dependent on how interested the reader is in the setting.

Don't go overboard. Usually, a seemingly insignificant, tiny sensory cue can be more powerful than two paragraphs of lazy, verbose description. A skipping record player, repeating the same line over and over because an unconscious butler is laying across it. A room where your hero's each footstep crunches because thieves have been tossing peanut shells to the ground. A martial arts studio which has heated floors, after the Korean style, that warm bare feet during the fight. These kinds of simple, yet dense, descriptions can be unique, evocative, and—most important—immersive, yet can still be conveyed in an economy of words.

Let's go through that opening fight sequence again, this time adding some real, concrete detail and giving the scene some uniqueness. I'm going to take this scene into a more modern setting with my descriptions, as for this exercise, I don't have the space to lay the framework of a solid, fantastical setting. In this way, my example can be somewhat generic so that it can be applied to any type of writing you may do.

Keep in mind, however, that these principles are just as important in fantasy as in realistic fiction—perhaps even more so, since many setting details can't be taken for granted. If you've got dragons fighting in midair, you still want to establish where the dragons are in relation to each other and the ground. Your heroic magician still needs to know where everyone is before he can fling spells.

Jim burst through the doors to the hideout. The old kitchen inside was lit by dusty lamps that hung from long chains. They swayed softly as a train rumbled across the nearby tracks. The air still bore hints of garlic and oregano from the foods that had once cooked here.

There were eight of Suro's men inside; thugs with slab-like faces and brutish features. Six sat at a table scattered with cards and folded bills. The two lounging by the doorway jumped back, uttering exclamations of surprise.

Jim punched one of the door guards with a loose jab—his knuckles popping against the man's jaw—then spun and roundhoused the thug on the other side, slamming him into the wall. The thug went down with a crunch; Jim couldn't tell if it was bone or wood that had cracked. He

*turned back to the first thug and knocked
the knife from the man's hand, then buried
a fist in the man's gut, then dropped him.
The wooden floorboards trembled as the
guard hit the floor.*

You can see that we're getting longer with each
iteration. This is okay; if we're doing our job correctly,
the story will actually read more quickly despite the
increased length. This phenomenon is something to be
aware of, however. Detail and scene-setting both take
extra space. Generally, I'd suggest planning on a few
stronger sequences than a large number of shorter, weaker
sequences. A few good fights can go a long way.

Our scene with Jim isn't done yet; it still has the feel
of a dressed up blow-by-blow. It's getting closer, but we
still need a final touch, a last bit of depth.

PRINCIPLE THREE: CHARACTER

Writers often expect that the nature of a fight sequence
will make it interesting by default. Because the heroes are
(presumably) in danger, writers assume tension will be
maintained naturally.

This assumption is true, to an extent, *if* you've laid
your groundwork (i.e., you've built strong rooting interest
for your characters and have established a real sense of
danger). However, sometimes you can't lay this
groundwork—such as when you start the book with the
action sequence. In addition, I don't feel that rooting
interest is enough to prevent readers from skipping a bad
sequence.

And so, we come to my final suggestion—the one that
may well be the fundamental trick to writing good action
sequences. It has to do with remembering the strengths of
prose, as opposed to other kinds of storytelling. We have
the awesome ability to put a reader *directly* into a

character's head, give the reader direct thoughts, motivations, and emotions.

The most powerful fights I've read in books have been the ones where every moment—every description, every punch—is channeled through the motives, emotions, and goals of the hero. Obviously, an action scene isn't the time for your hero to sit down and ponder the philosophy of identity. However, just a few character cues added to a sequence can change it dramatically.

Don't let the reader forget *why* your hero is fighting. Don't let them forget what he or she is trying to achieve. These are the threads that bind the reader to the page and truly inspire a sense of danger and tension.

In this, books have a huge advantage over film. Yes, we have to give labored descriptions of scenes they can paint with a three-second panning shot. Yes, they can maintain audience interest through inherent motion and visual action. But we can give you the why *and make you really feel it*. The audience of a film gets to watch the hero; we can make our readers *be* the hero.

Make sure to use this; don't ignore your greatest strength. Take out some of your blow-by-blow hitting; you don't need as much of it as you think. Replace it with fighting that is personal to the hero, showing motivations through careful hints and expressions of emotion and thought.

Your viewpoint character should be the lens through which the story is experienced. And in a fight, a time of passion—anger, pain, tension, motion—is when it's most important to give us solid characterization. Here is one more revision of our scene from the beginning of the essay.

Jim burst through the doors to the old, worn-out kitchen. The room was lit— poorly—by two dusty lamps that hung from long chains and swayed softly as a train rumbled across the nearby tracks. The air bore hints of garlic and oregano; it smelled like his mother's own kitchen had, long ago.

There were eight of Suro's men here, their hair slicked back, wearing tight shirts underneath sports coats. Suro liked his thugs to look like...well, anything but thugs. Seeing them made Jim sick; dressing men like them in suits was like dropping a handful of dung on a nice, silk handkerchief.

Suro himself sat at the end of the table scattered with cards, an incense punk hanging from his lips, the tip sending a curling line of smoke into the air. The room was pungent with the spicy scent. Suro didn't smoke *them, really. He just liked to chew on the ends as they smoldered in front of his face.*

Jim forced down his anger upon seeing the man, banishing images of Limi's bloodied lips and lifeless eyes. There was no time for reflection. The twins—Dak and Moe—lounged by the doorway, probably trading insults, as they usually did. They were dangerous. Very dangerous.

But, fortunately, they weren't terribly clever. Jim tossed his half-eaten apple toward Dak.

"Skata!" Dak cursed in his thick accent as he ducked the apple. It hadn't been meant to hit, just distract.

Were you there when she cried in pain, Moe? *Jim thought, bringing his fist around toward the other twin's face.* Did you listen to her pleas for mercy?

Moe ducked back by reflex, eyes wide, reaching for his coat pocket. Jim sprang forward and caught the man's necktie—it flapped in the air following Moe's dodge—

then yanked it forward. Moe urked, *eyes bugging as he stumbled. Jim's fist took him in the jaw.*

Moe dropped, the flimsy floorboards rattling beneath Jim's feet. No time to stop, no time to stop. *He could weep later. He could rest later.*

He could die later.

Jim spun, taking Dak in the gut with a roundhouse. The man had been staring at the apple, dumbfounded, as if he'd been expecting a grenade. Dak crunched back against the doorframe, causing it to shake, dust sprinkling down.

Jim drew in a ragged breath. His fatigue was draining away, fading before his fury. Thirty-six hours without sleep, but only a few more minutes until vengeance. He turned toward the center of the room.

The sounds of the train grew distant. The incense punk dropped from Suro's stunned lips and hit the table, singing a card, scattering ash. Only a few heartbeats had passed.

Jim dashed for the table as Suro finally yelled a belated "Get him!" to the other dumbfounded thugs.

Notice that in this final version of the sequence, the actual fighting takes a back seat to Jim's motivations and emotions. Our story stops being about the fighting and starts being about the hero, and within that context, the fight becomes far more interesting and personal.

I feel that many writers get this backward; that the action makes the hero. No. The hero makes the action. Even in cinema, we're not so interested in what James Bond, Aragorn, or Luke Skywalker is doing as we are *who* is doing it. In the final sequence above, we try to show Jim's thought process—he considers what he needs to do, though does so quickly.

As the sequence would progress, we could ease away from this and into some more focus on the fighting. The deeper you get into the action sequence, the fewer motivation, character, and setting clues you'll need. (Though you shouldn't stop them entirely.)

Just make sure the scene doesn't go too long; if it does go more than a few pages, pull back and give a breather, then re-establish, and re-cement the reader into the scene with more setting and character. Then shift back to fighting.

You might notice that in the scene above, I also revised to give the fight a little more variety. Suro has a quirk, the men by the door have names and personalities, and we do things like use the apple and the necktie to play with expectations and use the setting as part of our fighting.

When you write, each few lines should try to do something innovative, attempt something slightly out of the ordinary. When you can show a character being clever—or considering their surroundings, or making connections and using them in the midst of the battle—it will make a scene more engaging. This is because your reader won't lose sight of character, and will get to experience variety and flavor with each line.

Another tip is to use sentence length and variety to your advantage. Short sentences will feel like a clipped staccato. Long sentences will feel smoother. Don't get it the other way around—a lot of new writers assume that short means fast. That's not always the case; a lot of short sentences can give a feel of focus, but their clipped nature can actually slow the reader down.

A single sentence paragraph slows them even more.

The single-sentence paragraph is a moment of revelation or change. A literary punch to the face. I suggest not overusing it, for if you do any one thing in large quantities the readers will adapt to it and it will lose its effect.

The most important thing, however, is not to assume that your fight scenes will be interesting just because they are fight scenes. Try to imbue each one with the same quirks and variety that you give your heroes themselves. And remember, the fight sequence *can't* just be about the fight. Give your readers a reason to care about who is getting hit, give them a place for the hitting to happen, and give them a pinch of ingenuity in each and every scene and your action sequences will stand with the best of them.

Watching from the Sidelines

CAT RAMBO

Heroes, whether starring in heroic fantasy or some other genre, don't exist in a vacuum. They aren't a single stick figure standing in the middle of an otherwise blank page. In reality (if we can ever use that word when talking about fiction), they're the center of a web of relationships: familial, economic, desire-based, and otherwise shaped by physical circumstance.

That's why, while your story requires an antagonist, it also requires an array of supporting characters: family members, servants, friends, confidantes, allies, and others. These aren't simply cardboard cut-outs stuck in to supply the story's need—each one is potential to be mined. The more realized these characters are in the author's head, the more they have to contribute to the story.

Among the story assets these characters supply is a useful lens through which to present the protagonist, one that allows the writer to do three things:

- ✦ Accomplish extra world building.
- ✦ Make the main character more engaging.
- ✦ Supply additional story details.

My story "Eyes Like Sky and Coal and Moonlight" (Paper Golem LLC, 2009) is a useful example when talking about this approach. The tale takes it to an extreme by focusing on one of these side characters, letting her narrate her small version of the story, and

Cat Rambo

59

letting the reader glimpse only bits and pieces of the larger one.

The story, told from the point of view of someone who is affected by, rather than affecting, the events around her, becomes the larger story in miniature, one that shows it in a refracted and sometimes skewed style dependent on the reader's surmises about the offstage action.

"Eyes Like Sky and Coal and Moonlight" provides this take on world-changing events enacted by the ostensible heroine the narrator is observing: Alkyone.

This choice of narrator allowed me to take huge events—a war, a rebellion, the devastation of a city—and show their effect on a side character who, like the reader, does not know exactly how events have played out at the highest level. The overall grand story arc comes in scattered rumors:

> *My ineffectual efforts at magic died out after a while and our lives continued. When I was twelve, there came rumors of magic outside the city. Travelers reported the undead walked the North Road at night, and no one dared journey beneath the moons. Day by day, the stories grew wilder. They said an ancient demon, the Lord of Ash, and his servants plagued Tuluk and that the Templarate could do nothing to stop him. Others went further and said that the reason the Templarate did nothing was that they had given their power to Lord Isar.*
>
> *...*
>
> *Months later, though, I was vindicated when travelers spoke of the night the lights had flashed in the sky to mark the last battle with the Lord of Ash. They said Alkyone helped defeat him, but that it was a joint effort, really—the J'Karr and the*

Tan Muark, and a handful of magickers joined together. That their dead friend Arianis had come back as a gwoshi to help them defeat the Lord of Ash, that there had been a fierce fight nonetheless, and Kul had offered no aid—he'd been off in the North on his own expedition, searching for ways to defeat Isar.

They said down in the Salt Flats there was just a statue of the Lord of Ash, what he had been, turned into black stone— obsidian. My eldest once traveled down to see it, and said it was large and wicked, and that she dreamed of it for three nights running. The Muark still make the trip there once a year, to piss on its feet and curse it.

Because, honestly, how often can we read the story of the Chosen One, who saves a world, without starting to wonder about the circumstances surrounding them? Isn't it more interesting to look at it through the perspective of why those crazy Muark travel down to pee on a statue's feet in a yearly ritual?

So in "Eyes Like Sky and Coal and Moonlight," I've looked at the main story through the eyes of a character who is unnamed, who starts with the small details of a night when revolution foments:

Smell the storm brewing this evening—that edge of lightning riding the wind? That's how it smelled that first night they came. Everyone in the tavern was alive and electric that night. Word had spread there was to be a secret meeting of those who opposed Lord Isar.

The commons were packed to the gills

with Tan Muark and Tuluki followers of Kul. Everyone called him Kul, despite his rank, as high as that of Lord Isar. Everyone thought of him as a distinguished friend, an elder brother. The one who would defend us all.

The choice of this narrator, an innkeeper's child, allows me to supply detail after detail, particularly sensory ones. I've filtered details of the experience through her child-keen senses. Alkyone is a wind-mage and the "edge of lightning riding the wind" presages her appearance. And the narrator speaks in child-like similes, "a distinguished friend, an elder brother."

There's something about the narrator's position in relation to the overall story that lets me build up this sort of layering of detail in a way that would feel draggy or bulky and somewhat overanxious if attached to the actual protagonist. Details like a child's portrait of the economics of Allanak:

Wonders came from the southern city of Allanak: obsidian bracelets, and puppets with joints carved from bone. And sticky dried insects laced with honey that came in big blocks so chunks could be pried off to be chopped and added to pastries. I said this.

Or the incense and steak-nostalgia of:

The night winds were howling, and my mother lit thick cones of lanturin incense to keep away ghosts. In the middle of the meal—duskhorn steak, the wild-fed kind you can never get nowadays—the main door blew open, or so we thought at first. The youngest children were all screaming and things were confused. My mother

glimpsed Alkyone's form huddled outside,
a few feet away from the lintel. My
brothers pulled her in, dragged her beside
the hearth, pressed hot tea and soup on
her. She kept her eyes turned down, her
cloak's hood drawn up.
    A few hours later, her friends arrived.
They stood in the doorway. She did not
look up. No one had wanted to go to bed
after that, not with all the excitement, and
my father had allowed us to heat watered
wine and drink it, stretching out the sips to
make our time awake as long as possible.

Part of that is my tribute to one of the books that informed my childhood reading—*Little House in the Big Woods*. I know it seems like an odd thing to be informing heroic fantasy, but for me heroic fantasy was an important component of childhood and supplied many of the narratives that let me make my way through its tribulations. *LHitBW* is full of the sensory and the details that matter to a child, such as strategies for escaping bedtime.

    At the same time this choice allows me an additional relationship between my main character and someone else (the narrator) that (I hope) makes her more engaging and human. Alkyone is kind to the child narrator when they first meet, in ways that shows she still has empathy for the things that matter to children. Someone who understands children is often appealing to the reader. It's someone who, we think, would understand the child part of ourselves.

    Alkyone's first act is one of welcome, her second that of generosity, her third an act of bonding through speech.

She smiled at me and shared her honey
cakes, crumbling them with long, nervous
fingers. Her accent was lilting as she told

*me she had never had honey cakes when
she was growing up.*

Alkyone gives the narrator the earrings that will let
her recognize her in their final encounter in a moment that
foreshadows her conflicts with Phaedrin, his attempts to
master and direct her. At the same time, this passage
shows that she's already moving toward the story's final
moments, preparing herself by "lightening her pack."

> *One of the men filling the room muscled
> his way through the crowd. He was blonde
> bearded, a northerner like me. As he
> approached, he scowled down at me, but
> spoke to her.*
> *"What are you up to, Alkyone?" he
> said.*
> *"Lightening my pack," she said. "It
> has been heavy lately."*
> *"We can't afford to be giving away
> things all over the place," he said. "Come
> in the back room, they wish to know what
> our magics are capable of, and whether
> yours could carry someone outside the
> gate despite themself."*
> *I opened the box and he spoke as I saw
> what lay inside, "Those are your favorite
> earrings, Alk!"*
> *She put her head down, looking at the
> floor planks between her boot toes. "I had
> those before we ever met, Phaedrin. My
> friend Jhiran gave them to me, and I may
> give them where I will."*

In the end, even though Alkyone has been exiled from
her chosen home and knows that she is about to die,
saying "I have but a day in this form before I am returned
to the wind," she gives her moments to the narrator one
last time:

At the door, she stopped, seeing me. "I recognize those earrings. Is all well with you?" She waved the men on ahead.

"The inn is still standing—we lost the stable and some livestock," I said. "And my little sister's barrakhan pen, which is why we have no eggs."

The words were inconsequential. I drank the sight of her in. Her eyes were no longer coal. They were the color of moonlight on the sands. They were sad, but they were so beautiful that they gave me hope, if that makes sense.

The side character can supply additional details of the story, ones that the main character may never see, such as the details of Tuluk's devastation, reduced to the matters that concern the narrator the most: the cheese the family eats while waiting to find out if they and the inn will be destroyed, the block of buildings around the inn, and Lisette's death.

That night, elementals walked through the city, beings from planes outside our own. The city shook with their passage all night long. We hid in the cellar with four crates of Reynolte wine and a keg of spiced brandy. The Tan Muark had brought up a great wheel of cheese on their unexpected visit two days earlier, and we ate half of it that night because there wasn't anything else to do.

I wondered where Alkyone was. Surely she was part of this? Had the Lord of Ash returned, was she out there helping defeat him once again? Who had brought the elementals to destroy the city? Were her

Cat Rambo

65

friends with her still, was exiled Kul there to defend his home? Did she remember giving me her honey cakes, back when I was as old as the child huddled against me?

And what color were her eyes now?

It was a long night and none of us slept, only sat awake listening to the cries and feeling the earth shake whenever some monstrous thing passed in the street outside, nibbling at our cheese as though it would quiet the nervous snakes in our stomachs.

In the morning, the city was gone.

Our inn still stood, but other buildings near us had been burned and flattened.

Survivors recounted stories of a great fire-winged hawk from the plane of Suk-Krath, and a stone tortoise from Ruk, and a girl made of water from Vivadu. Liselle was dead. They wouldn't let me see the body, but I heard the whispers. The water elemental had drowned her with a kiss.

Many of the details this narrator supplies are based around her experience as a member of the merchant class:

Rumors said Kul was in exile. He'd tried to kill Isar after retrieving some artifact, and had been driven to live with the Tan Muark. Some people said he'd married a Muark woman who'd fallen in battle a few days later. We did not see the tribe much after that, and you couldn't get blue silk ribbons for years. They were the only ones with the secret of the dye.

Because they're so close to the action, your main character may not be the best point of view to operate from. A side character can observe a hero's frailty with affection, derision, or awe. They can supply dialogue and play Sancho Panza to their Don Quijote moments.

Pick your side characters and consider at least slipping into their heads from time to time. They may supply unexpected details of or insights into the main character.

Particularly at the end of a story, such a side character may provide a way to pull the camera back slowly from the main character in a move that helps establish to the reader that this is the end of the story.

> *I'll always remember her eyes. All through my life, through the betrayals and petty rivalries, the moments that were large and small and everything in between, the thought of her eyes has gotten me through the hard times. She walked by herself, and gave me the strength to do it as well, by remembering her eyes. Not as they were at first, a storybook blue, the color of the ancient days when it rained, and certainly not when they burned with that black, fierce light.*
>
> *But rather as they were that final night, when she walked out in the company of the gentle evening wind, a fearless woman who had given all she could in the fight and who would never be seen again. Her remarkable eyes, silver as the moonlight, and twice as kind, and a thousand times as brave and alone.*

Think as well about what the side character thinks about the main character, how their encounters with each other have shaped the side character's life. This is the lens which, at one level, we use to observe the narrator's life.

Alkyone is important to her. Memories of her heroism, her actions and words, allow the narrator to carry on through her darkest moments:

> *For years afterwards, I could take my breath away just thinking of her eyes. It took me through some hard times—later the occupation by the Allanaki, and when my two youngest were killed by the Borsail lord they'd sent up to oversee things. We didn't know it then, that we'd be decades under their heel because of what the elementalists had done. But I never hated her, never thought that even when they were taking my children.*
>
> *The rebels kidnapped the Lord's son and he swore that for every day the child was not in his nurse's arms, twenty Northern babies would die. They took mine on the third day, and would have taken another, except I lied and said he was too old—had seen over three years now. I thought of her eyes, and they gave me strength to say the falsehood flatly, as though there was no way it could be anything but true. You do what you can and see what happens.*

Heroic fantasy tries to supply such figures, heroes who, through their courage, their actions, motivate us to do the heroic in turn. That's a central theme in "Eyes Like Sky and Coal and Moonlight," the effect of the hero on the observer. It requires heroes to start a revolution sometimes, and it will be a revolution not of individual heroes and figures of legends but of the masses, as represented by the narrator, that will lead to the overthrow of those oppressing the city of Tuluk. At the same time, those masses and their exemplar, our unnamed narrator, are inspired by the stories of heroes, such as the very one the narrator is being urged by some unguessed at interlocutor (A spy? One of the bards of the new Poets Circle? A grandchild? A fellow traveler?) to tell.

Which is, at the highest level, what stories of heroic fantasy are about—the inspiration of the hero in us all and the impetus to help us live our lives, just as the narrator lives hers in "Eyes Like Sky and Coal and Moonlight."

Man Up:
Making your Hero an
Adult

ALEX BLEDSOE

There's a quintessential image in fantasy: the idealistic youth looking up into the sky and off into the future, his gleaming sword raised as a challenge to the world. It's Arthur after drawing Excalibur from the stone or Luke Skywalker on the original Hildebrandt poster for *Star Wars*.

If you're reading this, though, you're probably more interested in the older, battle-hardened and cynical hero standing in a wasteland surrounded by the bodies of his adversaries, his bloody sword held wearily at his side. This is Conan, Kull, or Elric, and it's the opposite of the idealistic youth. And for me, it's is a far more interesting character: I prefer to both read and write stories about grown men and not untested boys.

But in the broader fantasy genre, there's an abiding interest in the immature hero forced—by circumstances or that catch-all term 'destiny'—to essentially 'man up' and save the day. Frodo in *The Lord of the Rings* is such a character. The most popular example is Luke Skywalker, simple farm boy who turns out to be the 'new hope' of the galaxy. Thanks to George Lucas and his very public embrace of Joseph Campbell's work, as well as the growth of the Young Adult genre, it sometimes seems like fantasy consists of nothing but this story retold against different backgrounds. We've seen countless heroes, from

Luke Skywalker to Harry Potter to Percy Jackson, become men. We're hardly ever shown what happens next.

So I'm writing about the hero as a grown man. And I'm using male examples, but the issues are genderless: they apply if you're writing about Conan or Xena. I'll also be using examples mainly from movies, because film is a more common frame of reference, and it takes less time to watch a movie than read a book. And I'm not trying to tell you *how* to write, but to get you thinking about *what* you write in a new way.

INTRODUCTION

When establishing an older character, it's best to be clear up front. There are ways to do this without blatantly saying, "John Doe, 45 years old, drew his sword." Many things immediately mark an older man: wrinkles, gray hair, scars, even a certain world-weary bearing. An acceptable variation might be, "John Doe scratched his salt-and-pepper beard, then drew his sword." Simply by describing one physical trait, you have implied the character's age. Now you have to define him.

When I introduced my hero Eddie LaCrosse in *The Sword-Edged Blonde* (Night Shade Books, 2007), I tried to establish his age (late thirties) in a couple of hopefully subtle ways. One was in his narrative voice: since Eddie is telling the story, his attitude comes through in both the narration and the dialogue. He mentions that *back then* he worked out of a tavern office, and later says:

> *I leaned back and laced my fingers together over my stomach, which seemed larger than the last time I'd done so.*

Both those comments lend a sense of a man past youth, though not yet ready for the graveyard.

The other way was his ability to judge the first character he encounters in the story. Because of his own varied and extensive history, he recognizes the elderly messenger as:

> *...about sixty, thin and frail-looking, but with traces of a much larger, stronger man left in the set of his jaw and the way he sat up sharply each time he caught himself slumping. A soldier once, maybe even a high-ranking officer, now reduced to an errand boy.*

Thus within the first four pages, I hope the reader gets a sense of Eddie's maturity, intelligence and ability to correctly evaluate situations, all of which set him (and other heroic fantasy heroes) apart from the multitude of young warriors.

So once you've established your hero as an older man, there are three broad areas in which his personality significantly differs from that of a young man with a sword. They are: battles, women and vices.

BATTLES

So your hero stands, sword in hand, facing the villain. Now what? The younger hero might say something like, "You have met your match today, Lord Vile," or "Prepare to be skewered like a pig, Baron Worthless." Younger characters, untested and unproven, often feel the need to assert themselves in this way. It's a form of bragging, something to make them sound like more than they are, the equivalent of a frilled lizard or puffer fish display. Whether they live up to their claims, or suffer ignominious defeat, is up to the author.

The older hero, though, has proven his skills and toughness to the one person who matters most: himself. In the DVD audio commentary for *Escape from New York*, star Kurt Russell and director John Carpenter discuss their decision to make Snake Plissken so tough, all his fights are very short. The unspoken psychological basis for this is that Plissken no longer has anything to prove, and is all about getting the job done. This is a characteristic of the veteran hero, and it can be played for humor, suspense or out-and-out mayhem (as in *Yojimbo*, when Toshiro Mifune single-handedly slaughters a dozen samurai tough-guys and then claims a whole gang of killers did it).

But what if you decide your hero does need to speak; what sort of thing would he say? At this point in his life, he not only has no need to boast, he knows it's counterproductive. What's the opposite of a boast, then? A warning. So your hero might say something like, "This is a really bad idea, Lord Vile." Or, "Baron Worthless, is this truly necessary?" The words are both literally true, and subtly convey the fact that our villain might be getting in over his head. Whereas a challenge from a young hero might strike the villain as empty chest-thumping, this type of statement—which carries implications of skill, experience, and knowledge—might, or damn well should, give the villain pause. It establishes hero and villain as equals at best, and at worst gives the hero a subtle psychological advantage: after all, the villain feels no need to warn anyone ahead of time. How confident must the hero be if he feels he must?

So our hero and villain are facing off, swords drawn, and it's time for them to fight. There are two possible extremes, and I'll use examples from two very different films.

First is the endless, pointless duel that does nothing but prove the two characters are evenly matched. The dual between Jack Sparrow and Barbossa at the climax of *Pirates of the Caribbean: The Curse of the Black Pearl* is just that sort of thing, and it's rendered even more moot by the fact that both opponents are undead zombies and therefore can't be killed by the other (a fact Barbossa mentions). So there is no story purpose to the fight. Similarly, the final interminable duel in *Star Wars*

Episode III: Revenge of the Sith has no narrative point because the audience already knows who wins.

At the other extreme is *Sanjuro*, in which Toshiro Mifune faces off—literally—against Tatsuya Nakadai. The two stand almost face to face, unmoving, for a full 45 seconds, before Mifune suddenly draws his sword and skewers his opponent in a move so fast it's almost unbelievable (and done in real time, too). The duel resolves both the story and the thematic issue of seeing the truth behind someone's public face.

As I said, these are extremes. Between them are limitless opportunities. In *Burn Me Deadly* (Tor Books, 2009), Eddie LaCrosse finds himself faced with two dozen bad guys, most of whom are not trained warriors. First he tries to talk his way out:

> *"Fellas, I said genially. "There seems to be some misunderstanding here. I don't want any trouble; I'm just passing through."*

Unfortunately he's recognized, but he continues to try to avoid a fight.

> *"Hey, be reasonable. I'm sorry I had to punch you, but things happen. Would money make you feel better?"*

Only when this fails, and the bad guys produce weapons, does he concede to fight. He decimates them quickly and efficiently, and with a fair bit of regret.

You also have additional elements you can add to the mix. Consider the young hero's desire to show off. More than likely he'd wave his sword, twirl it, display his mastery with a series of moves that are totally useless in an actual fight. He might laugh, or mock his opponent. What he probably won't do is take the time to seriously discern his opponent's skills before diving into the fray.

Alex Bledsoe

75

A mature hero knows better. In *The Princess Bride* both Inigo and Westley begin their epic sword battle fighting left-handed, putting themselves at a disadvantage because each believes himself far superior to the other. Only when they realize they are evenly matched do they switch to their dominant right hands. A veteran might use a similar tactic, pretending to be a worse fighter than he actually is in order to measure the weaknesses of his opponent. Or he might simply fight defensively, using as little energy as possible, and wait for his opponent to tire and show a vulnerable spot.

The crucial difference is in the hero's mind. A young hero is out to prove something; a veteran is trying to do a job. And as the author, that's where you make your hero unique.

Which brings us to...

WOMEN

Every story's hero—and for the sake of expediency, I'm considering 'hero' to also mean 'heterosexual male,' although the issues can apply to any gender or combination the author wishes—eventually needs a companion, and often this means a woman. In heroic fantasy, there are two types: the ones that need the hero's protection, and the ones that stand at his side as equals. Both can be powerful characters, but how the hero relates to them is critical in establishing his maturity (or lack of it).

The young hero does not want an equal. His unformed ego couldn't stand it. He's either convinced of his own uniqueness, or desperately trying to convince himself of it. The heroine, then, has value only in how she supports him. Usually she's the damsel in distress, the princess in the tower, the sleeping beauty under glass. Her presence at the story's end makes her a living, breathing testament to the hero's success. And to paraphrase David Gerrold, of course she loves him: it's her *job*.

One of the best examples of this dynamic, and its inversion, is found in John Steinbeck's unfinished retelling of King Arthur. In the "Gawain, Ewain and Marhalt" section of *The Acts of King Arthur and his Noble Knights*, the three warriors in question meet three magical ladies, and they pair off to have a year's worth of adventures. Crucially, the women see the knights for exactly who and what they are, while the knights see only prizes (Gawain goes the whole year without even asking his companion's name).

But here's where Steinbeck uses our knowledge of the genre to fool us. The youngest of the knights, Ewain, is joined by the *oldest* of the ladies, Lyne. He at first believes she, at "threescore" (i.e., sixty) years, has fallen in love with his youth. Instead, she has seen the possibility in him, and takes it on herself to train him to become the best knight he can. At first Ewain can't even process this sort of relationship, but eventually he comes to appreciate her wisdom, and to heed her teaching.

The mature hero has different priorities. Secure in his self-knowledge, he is not threatened by an equal, but rather welcomes it. In *Burn Me Deadly*, Eddie LaCrosse awakens after a beating to find his girlfriend Liz at his bedside:

> *She wore a tight tunic blouse and men's-style trousers with high boots. Her short red hair was matted and strands fell into her equally red eyes. The harsh light from the window highlighted the crow's-feet and smile lines on her face. She needed a bath, a change of clothes and some serious rest. I thought she was the most beautiful sight in the world.*

I wrote the scene this way because I wanted to show that Eddie both saw Liz clearly, and yet loved her so much he found her beautiful even at her worst. And the subsequent dialogue deliberately works against this romanticism, to provide balance:

> *"Do you go out in public like that?" I asked.*
> *"You're no picnic yourself. And watching you sleep is just as exciting as it sounds."*

This ability to evaluate a romantic partner is as important as understanding the danger presented by a villain. So let's say your hero comes upon a beautiful woman in a glade, tied to a tree and clearly about to be, as the euphemism goes, 'ravished.' The young hero would leap immediately to the lady's defense, freeing her and battling her would-be ravisher. The veteran, though, might hang back and take in the situation in more detail, perhaps discovering that the woman, far from being a victim, is merely the bait in a trap. Or, if still held against her will, that perhaps she had done something to merit this treatment. The point is, he would not instantly assume the situation was as it first appeared.

If the lady *is* a victim, he would certainly rescue her. That leaves the question of payment. No doubt she is young and beautiful, properly virginal, and aware that her beauty is both her blessing and curse. The young hero would swear undying love, possibly even marry her, only to find he'd jumped when he should've run. The mature hero, older and wiser, might accept 'payment' but certainly wouldn't fall in love and risk his freedom simply because a woman happened to be attractive. Moreover, should she fall in love with him, he would make certain she harbored no illusions about a potential future.

So if our adult hero isn't interested in beautiful princesses, what sort of woman might attract him? One who asked nothing from him that conflicts with his personal standards, and who expects nothing from him but honesty. She would accept what he could give, ask for no more than that, and he would show her the same courtesy.

Now before you lash me for being sexist, let's go back to the movies and look at an example of this sort of relationship. First the negative: *Casablanca*. Humphrey Bogart must choose between duty and Ingrid Bergman. Duty wins. Cue "La Marseillaise." But then we take a look at *To Have and Have Not*. Once again, Bogart is the lone American in a foreign city. Once again he's carefully neutral, not interested in the world war playing out around him. And once again there's a beautiful girl (Lauren Bacall this time), whose presence ultimately forces him to choose sides. But in this case, the dynamic is totally different. Marie, a.k.a. Slim, is as tough as Bogart, as quick-witted and resourceful, and proves herself in a crisis. He'd be an idiot to nobly leave her behind, and he doesn't even try: they go off to win World War II together. Slim is the prototype, in fact, for the mature hero's perfect woman.

And at last we come to...

VICES

The young hero's vices are all internal, things innately a part of his personality. Pride is the real danger: the certainty that comes with youth can, in a sword-and-sorcery character, prove fatal very quickly. He may be the best-trained swordsman in the shire, but unless Lord Vile plays by the same rules, he's at a serious disadvantage. The greatest lesson the young hero must learn is to see the world as it is, not how it's supposed to be.

The veteran hero knows this without even consciously thinking about it. He may drink, even to excess, but not when there's work to do. He knows that lowering his guard is the most dangerous thing possible, so he will patronize trusted venues where he's safe. And even then, he'll sit in the corner and keep one eye on the door. He's survived being the younger boy, drunk for the first time and helplessly passed out, and he knows that only dumb luck or the generous protection of someone else got him through. He certainly won't provoke a fight when his own reflexes and skills are numbed by drink; and if someone tries to provoke him, he'll give them every chance to back down.

The one who usually provokes a fight in this situation is ironically the young hero, who sees insult to his honor in every comment when he's sober, let alone when he's drunk for the first time. He also—and this is a crucial difference—has no understanding of the way drink impairs his skills. If anything, drink makes him believe he's more invincible than ever. The modern term would be, 'ten feet tall and bullet-proof.' If he survives, it's usually because his opponent recognizes his condition and refuses to take advantage of him (think Yul Brynner and Horst Buchholz in *The Magnificent Seven*). If he doesn't survive, he's remembered as a fool.

I gave Eddie LaCrosse a history of vices, but by the time the first novel picks him up, he's put most of them behind him. Still, the attraction remains, as I tried to convey in this passage from *Dark Jenny* (Tor Books, 2011):

> *The [mercenary] camp smells assailing me—sweat, mud, urine, burning meat, and metal—brought back memories I'd hoped to repress until my old age. And the worst part was, not all of them were unpleasant. When I saw two men laughing over their tankards as they sat beside a fire, I remembered the hours I'd spent doing the same thing, telling bullshit stories and calling bullshit on other people's.*

Then there are women. These are not the same women as mentioned above, where the 'L' word might be spoken (although they certainly *may* be, but for the sake of this example, we're assuming not). Women who make themselves available to warriors tend to have few illusions about themselves, men or the world in general. They can also be as dangerous as any man with a sword. The veteran hero knows this, and if he indulges in this sort of thing, it's with the same boundaries as his drinking: with someone he's sure he can trust, but with one foot out the door, metaphorically speaking. He also makes sure he treats this woman with kindness and respect, understanding that the morality of her career choice is entirely hers. He makes no judgments.

In *The Sword-Edged Blonde*, I introduced this type of woman in Angelina, a sexy tavern keeper and Eddie's landlord:

> *Angelina was not young, although she was beautiful in a way that only grew stronger the more time you spent with her. She could've done much better for herself than owning this ratty tavern where she endured the occasional gropes and rudeness in return for respectable tips. I knew she was hiding out from something, but it was none of my business. We all have secrets.*

Young heroes can be as dazzled by this sort of woman as they are by the wealthy princess. While the noble girl might have money, beauty and social position on her side, this earthier sort has...well, sex. Young heroes are often as inexperienced with physical love as they are the emotional kind, and are just as vulnerable when in the throes of it. Added to this is the young hero's certainty that no woman can be a physical danger to him, and you've got as good a recipe for a short, bloody life as you'd have on the battlefield. If the young hero survives, and pays attention, he'll learn a few things from this sort of woman that he can apply the next time he encounters a princess.

The third vice is more subtle, and can often be misconstrued as a strength. Certainly Conan, the template for all heroic fantasy heroes, did not see it as a problem. That vice is enjoying mayhem. It's what happens when the young hero accumulates enough experience to survive most martial encounters, but never loses the childish delight that comes from them. He becomes the warrior as bully, who seeks combat as a kind of high. The problem with this—for the warrior, not the writer—is that he can often be torn from this mind-set by an unexpected event. The climax of Ib Melchoir's classic SF story "The Racer" is the perfect example of this (go find it in an anthology; I don't want to spoil it here). Both the young hero and the veteran can be forced to confront their own deeds from the perspective of their victims, something neither may have contemplated.

Usually, however, the veteran hero has a deeper understanding of things. He's seen enough death and destruction to know with certainty that there's no glamour to it, only the grim work for which he's suited. He looks on a fellow warrior's glee as distasteful and immature, even as he recalls his own youthful callowness. I created vicious characters in *The Sword-Edged Blonde* (Stan Carnahan) and *Burn Me Deadly* (Candora), and in *Dark Jenny* let Eddie talk about them explicitly:

> *There were freaks on both sides, of course: men (and occasionally women) who enjoyed any excuse for killing. They were easy to spot, tough to stop, and ultimately did everyone a favor by attracting attention while the rest of us did our jobs. Their kills were usually less than you'd think, because after a while no one would engage them. They spent the latter part of the battle striding among corpses looking for someone to fight.*

The best popular example of the veteran hero who keeps his vices in perspective is, of course, James Bond. He knows a little about everything (including butterfly collecting, if you believe *On Her Majesty's Secret Service*), but a lot about alcohol, weapons and women. A *lot*. And yet with rare exceptions, these prove no distraction to his job. He's never incapacitated by drink, never comes across a weapon or vehicle he can't handle, and as for women...well, as the song says, nobody does it better, right?

CONCLUSION

When writing about your hero, the most important thing to understand is what makes him do the things you have him do. Sending him on a quest to Mount Shudder to steal the McGuffin Stone from our old pal Lord Vile provides a fine narrative structure, but your readers will only become involved if your hero has a compelling personal reason for going. If you create a hero who is young and untested, who overcomes his own inexperience and learns to be a man in the process of the journey, then it's a perfectly fine story (and works for *Star Wars*, *Lord of the Rings*, *Harry Potter*, etc.) but it's not really heroic fantasy.

A heroic fantasy hero might undertake this quest, but his reasons would be different. You certainly couldn't appeal to his patriotism, or his desire to do 'the right thing.' You'd likely have to pay him, either with gold or something else of value, and he'd be alert for any double-cross. He'd complete his task efficiently, with little fanfare, unless he discovered that his employers had double-crossed him or left out a particularly important bit of information. If so, he would have no qualms about betraying them and resolving things in his own way (The best example of this, and of the concept of the veteran hero in general, may be *The Wild Bunch*. Ernest Borgnine tells William Holden, "That [giving your word] ain't what counts! It's who you give it *to*!").

And this is what readers love about him, and what compels writers to tell stories about him. While the 'hero's journey' will always remain a valid template because it reflects who we are, the 'post-journey hero' shows us as we hope we'd become. It's comforting to think we might be as tough, resourceful, clever and dangerous as Conan. We may identify with Luke Skywalker or Frodo, but we want to *be* Han Solo or Aragorn.

So when creating your hero and telling his adventures, don't be afraid to make him a grown-up, with experience and mileage under his sword belt. To quote disgraced guru Carlos Castenada, "Nobody is born a warrior, in exactly the same way that nobody is born an average man. We make ourselves into one or the other." And while the tale of the making can be thrilling, the tale of the made has its own unique thrills as well.

Two Sought Adventure

HOWARD ANDREW JONES

I learned the hard way (years of rejections) that before you can write any character successfully, you have to know who they are and what their likes and dislikes are, what they think, how they react, what they like to eat...almost everything. You should strive to know them so well that when you chance upon something about them you *haven't* figured out—their favorite drink, say, or how they ready themselves for bed—the answer is obvious to you. You have to inhabit the skin of your protagonists. Believe me, if you don't find them fascinating enough to spend time with, no one else will want to do so either. That's not to say you have to know the life history of every doorman or spear catcher who stumbles into your scene, but you certainly have to walk in the shoes of all of your main characters, and all of those who have any kind of substantial interaction with them. You can get a lot of great mileage out of a minor character with a little motivation who interacts with your protagonists, as opposed to having your heroes converse with a dull characteroid.

One of the ways Shakespeare reveals character is by having his protagonists converse with a variety of people. These interactions highlight different aspects of the central characters so that our understanding of them deepens. The bard is a fine model in all manner of ways, but relative to this discussion I should mention that one of his great strengths is bringing life to even minor players, like the two murderers of Henry VI in *Richard III*. When Henry confronts them, one of the fellows has an attack of conscience, which makes the other's deed all that more monstrous. A lesser writer wouldn't have bothered giving either of these one-scene characters personality or motivation.

If you have multiple heroes, then you'd better know them equally well: strengths, weaknesses, peculiarities. Since I'm assuming that you're interested in adventure fiction if you're reading advice from me, let me also assume that you're wanting your heroes to function as a team. That's good, but it's no fun watching a team work perfectly all the time. Design those heroes so that there's natural conflict built into their relationship—create rough edges so that there will be abrasions sometimes when they interact.

The first adventuring heroes I ever saw in action were Kirk, Spock, and McCoy. Some people leave McCoy out of the discussion and think the focus is about the friendship between Kirk and Spock, but if they do, they're missing a key ingredient. These three are the unit that makes the greater hero.

In lesser hands, and in popular mythology, Kirk is a simple action hero—maybe he's a little smarter than some, but he's mostly sly and he always has an eye for the ladies. In the strong episodes, notably almost all of those scripted in the first season of the original show, Kirk is a man of action who is also an intellectual. Having Spock and McCoy as his advisers allows the viewer to see the internal dilemmas Kirk is feeling acted out between Spock (intellectual) and McCoy (emotional/intuitive). Of course the best *Star Trek®* writers rounded these characters so that they became much more than cardboard representations of Kirk's internal concerns. But the two different understandings of the world as seen by Spock and McCoy are the genesis of the conflicts between the three characters and why, when they work together, great things get done. It is as though one super hero—or one fully realized human being, with intellect and intuition/emotion working together—is on the job.

There are a large number of fine Kirk/Spock/McCoy scenes, but since my primary focus in this essay is actually on how to portray two heroes working together, I want to excerpt a great scene from a relatively weak episode in the second season titled "Bread and Circuses." The *Enterprise* is exploring a parallel world where Rome never fell. Spock and McCoy are in a cell after having survived participation in a televised gladiatorial combat. They have no idea what has been done with the Captain. At the start of the scene, a fairly relaxed looking McCoy is watching Spock methodically examine the bars of the cell. Descriptive notes are from my transcription; I have no idea what the stage instructions were.

> *McCoy: (Genially) Angry, Mr. Spock, or frustrated perhaps?*
> *Spock: Such emotions are foreign to me, Doctor. I'm merely testing the strength of the door.*
> *McCoy: (Still kindly) For the fifteenth time.*
> *Spock: (Returns to inspecting the way the door is attached to the cell.)*
> *McCoy: Spock. (He stands up and walks close, looking a little awkward, as though he's uncomfortable with what he's about to say.) Spock, I...know we've had our disagreements. Maybe they're jokes, I dunno. As Jim says, we're not often sure ourselves sometimes (laughs self-consciously) but what I'm trying to say is—*
> *Spock: Doctor, I am seeking a means of escape. Will you please be brief.*
> *McCoy: (smiling) Well, what I'm trying to say is...you saved my life in the arena.*
> *Spock: (matter-of-factly) Yes, that's quite true.*

> *McCoy: (A beat—his expression falls and he snaps) I'm trying to thank you, you pointed eared hobgoblin!*
>
> *Spock: (A beat—he is briefly puzzled, then recovers.) Oh, yes, you humans have that emotional need to express gratitude. 'You're welcome' I believe is the correct response. (He turns away to continue his examination of the bars.) However Doctor, you must remember that I am entirely motivated by logic. The loss of our ship's surgeon, whatever I may think of his relative skill, would mean a reduction in the efficiency of the* Enterprise *and therefore—*
>
> *McCoy: You know why you're not afraid to die, Spock? You're more afraid of living. Each day you stay alive is just one more day you might slip and let your human half peak out. That's it, isn't it? Insecurity. Why, you wouldn't know what to do with a genuine, warm decent feeling.*
>
> *Spock: (This has hit home and, looking away, it takes Spock a moment to pull together and turn with aplomb and arched eyebrow to act as if nothing has happened.) Really, Doctor?*
>
> *McCoy: (Softening) I know. I'm worried about Jim too.*

Now a lot of the reason the scene works is because of the way Deforest Kelley and Leonard Nimoy carry it; Nimoy as Spock is clearly masking his own nervous energy and frustration by trying to be productive and methodical. The sudden shifts in tone are handled beautifully by Kelley, who plays McCoy as a kind-hearted man who can take sudden offense then immediately back step. But a lot of the power is there in the script as well, understated. McCoy realizes that Spock is hiding his emotions and decides to call Spock on it, but when he sees his shot went home, his expression softens and he admits what Spock is unwilling to say, that he is worried about what's happened to Kirk. They manage to communicate even if it's not in the way either of them is comfortable doing.

Fritz Leiber's famous rogues, Fafhrd and the Gray Mouser, are similar to Spock and McCoy in that they don't always work smoothly together. It's well noted that there is a city mouse/country mouse dichotomy between the men, but there is also one of regional difference— Fafhrd coming from the icy northlands and the Mouser from the warmer south—and size—Fafhrd being large and powerful, the Mouser being small and quick. Then, too, they differ in temperament, and not along stereotypical lines. While the Mouser is quick and sly, Fafhrd is no hulking dummy, though he can be stubborn. Both are cynical, but whereas the Mouser has a rather ironic modernist take on events, Fafhrd can be both superstitious and sentimental. Yet they are as close as brothers. They bicker and fight and sometimes even drift apart, but they stick together and when the going gets rough they trust one another, no questions asked. That doesn't mean that they can't be irritated with each other even as they're working together.

I could cite any number of wonderful bits from the long career of Fafhrd and the Gray Mouser, but one of my favorites comes from the moment in "When the Sea King's Away" when they are exploring a strange cavity beneath the ocean. A mysterious magical entity has created a tunnel through the water for them. The ocean is held up a few feet over their heads, but rolls on to the sides. Fafhrd, who is far less cautious, advances in with a torch, which is filling the area with smoke. There is plenty of phosphorescence to see by.

"Blubber brain!" the Mouser greeted him. "Put out that torch before we smother! We can see better without it. Oh, Oaf, to blind yourself with smoke for the sake of light!"

To the Mouser there was obviously only one sane way to extinguish the torch—jab it in the wet muck underfoot—but Fafhrd, though evidentially most agreeable to the Mouser's suggestion in a vacantly smiling way, had another idea. Despite the Mouser's anguished cry of warning, he casually thrust the flaming stick into the watery roof.

There was a loud hissing and a large downward puff of steam and for a moment the Mouser thought his worst dreads had been realized, for an angry squirt of water from the quenching point struck Fafhrd in the neck. But when the steam cleared it became evident that the rest of the sea was not going to follow the squirt, at least not at once, though now there was an ominous lump like a rounded tumor, in the roof where Fafhrd had thrust the torch, and from it water ran steadily in a stream thick as a quill, digging a tiny crater where it struck the muck below.

"Don't do that!" the Mouser commanded in unwise fury.

"This?" Fafhrd asked gently, poking a finger through the ceiling next to the dripping bulge. Again came the angry squirt, diminishing at once to a trickle, and now there were two blue bulges closely side by side, quite like breasts.

"Yes, that—not again," the Mouser managed to reply, his voice distant and high because of the self-control it took him *not to rage at Fafhrd and so perhaps provoke even more reckless probings.*

"Very well, I won't," the Northerner assured him. "Though," he added, gazing thoughtfully at the twin streams, "it would take those dribblings years to fill up this cavity."

These sorts of disagreements among friends are what I use to inform my own fiction, and discussions between my characters Dabir and Asim, the scholar and warrior adventuring their way through an 8th century Arabia replete with dark wizards and things man was not meant to know. Here's a short excerpt of Dabir and Asim's attempt to obtain some answers from a reluctant scholar ("Sight of Vengeance," *Black Gate 10*, 2007). They've had to force their way into his house.

From out of the dim hallway beyond the reception room came a hairy Turk, naked save for his vest and pants. In his hand he bore a huge curved saber.

I leapt into the hall and whipped out my blade. My blood sang! Here was the sort of challenge at which I excelled. Leave Dabir to his dusty books—swordcraft was my field of study.

"Begone!" he cried, and swung at my head.

Sparks flared in the gloom as I caught his sword against mine. He had strength in his wiry arms.

"We need answers, Asim!" Dabir cried from behind, which was a not-so-subtle admonition not to kill the fellow. Dabir had scolded me in the past for leaving no foe left alive to question. Doubtless he supposed that sparing an enemy is a

Howard Andrew Jones

simple matter when each is trying to behead the other with a sharpened four-foot length of metal.

Asim and Dabir may be loyal comrades, but they're often critical of each other, just as real friends might be. Yet I don't make every one of their waking moments a descent into bickering any more than Fritz Leiber did with Fafhrd and the Gray Mouser, or the script writers did with the original *Star Trek* characters. That would be like watching a married couple pick at each other. They should be free to criticize one another *to* one another, but they should depend upon one another as well. It's not just about moments of weakness—there should be moments of strength, of working together like a well-oiled team, of standing back-to-back when the chips are down. If they are among other adventurers or folk, it should be clear from their attitude and stance that these guys are *together.* There's a wonderful scene in one of the greatest *Star Trek* episodes, "The City on the Edge of Forever," (written by Harlan Ellison, revised by D.C. Fontana) where Kirk and Spock are confronted by Edith Keeler about exactly who they really are. They are trying to blend in to the New York of the 1930s as they search for Dr. McCoy, and the astute Keeler senses that they are out of place. Spock asks where she thinks they do belong and she answers: "You? At his side, as if you've always been there and always will." Even someone newly acquainted with these two senses the loyalty between them.

Anyone who's really serious about writing a pair of heroes should not only read the Lankhmar stories, but should watch and re-watch *Butch Cassidy and The Sundance Kid* for all of the fabulous interaction between the characters. Just after the opening scene of the movie, Butch and Sundance ride back to the hideout to discover one of the gang members is bucking for leadership. Butch is the erstwhile leader and Sundance his best friend, and while they're a part of the gang, it's clear from speech and attitude that Butch and Sundance are a tighter unit still than the rest of the group.

I could randomly open nearly any script page from *Butch Cassidy and The Sundance Kid* with dialogue and find a gem, but to provide a quick window into their relationship I've chosen the concluding moments of the movie, when Butch and Sundance are wounded and holed up in a small building in Bolivia, getting ready to make a dash for freedom. As anyone who's seen the movie knows, Butch and Sundance have no idea that the opposition outside is far more deadly than they anticipate. Butch, always more gregarious, hides his nerves with dialogue as they're peering out toward the sunset, planning their escape route.

> **Butch**: *I've got a great idea where we should go next.*
> **Sundance**: *Well I don't wanna hear it.*
> **Butch**: *You'll change your mind once I tell you—*
> **Sundance**: *Shut up.*
> **Butch**: *O.K.; O.K.*
> **Sundance**: *It was your great ideas got us here.*
> **Butch**: *Forget about it...*
> **Sundance**: *I never want to hear another of your great ideas, all right?*
> **Butch**: *All right.*
> **Sundance**: *Good.*
> **Butch**: *Australia.*
> **Sundance**: *(Looks darkly at Butch.)*
> **Butch**: *I figured secretly you wanted to know so I told you: Australia.*
> **Sundance**: *That's your great idea?*
> **Butch**: *The latest in a long line.*
> **Sundance**: *Australia's no better than here!*
> **Butch**: *That's all you know.*
> **Sundance**: *Name me one thing.*

Butch: They speak English in Australia.
Sundance: (Surprised) They do?
Butch: That's right, smart guy, so we wouldn't be foreigners. And they ride horses. And they got thousands of miles to hide out in—and a good climate, nice beaches, you could learn to swim—
Sundance: Swimming's not important; what about the banks?

That dialogue's great—it's almost criminal of me to stop typing it in, because I'm pretty sure you want to know what they're going to say next. If you've never seen the movie, or haven't seen it in a while, I strongly urge you to watch it if, for nothing else, to take in that beautiful character-driven dialogue that in turn drives the plot.

In this excerpt from the first Dabir and Asim novel, *The Desert of Souls* (Thomas Dunne Books, 2011), I would like to say that I kept these sorts of scenes in mind, but in truth I didn't model any of the conversation off of any of the preceding excerpts I've shown you. I created the characters in such a way that they clash sometimes even when they're working together. Every writer will have different tricks that may work better for him or her than they will for others, but I find that when I know my characters and their differences well, their dialogue pretty much writes itself.

That said, I wouldn't have known how to draft such a scene if I hadn't been paying attention to similar scenes and *listening to how real friends talk* the whole of my life.

In this chapter Dabir and Asim have been trapped in a magical realm by the sorcerer Firouz and are making their way through the place at night, encountering strange and peculiar things.

It was not too much longer before the sun gathered up the last of its colors and sank in a glorious bed of gold below the horizon. Then the stars came out and if there is one thing I could pluck from my mind's eye so that all might see, it is the sight of the stars glimmering there above the Desert of Souls. Although heavens are usually beautiful and clear in a desert, here they were impossibly glorious, flaming balls of different hues set in velvet folds of deepest indigo. No gold nor silver nor precious gems can equal the beauty of that vision and the words to describe that magnificent, splendid web of light do not exist, or at least cannot be commanded by this feeble hand.

Dabir and I agreed that the stars were an awesome sight. We admired them as they rose, and stared long at them as we walked, for they marked our route. Almost I was glad that we might be trapped there, to have seen such a thing. The moon gleamed, too, like a silver ball unmarred by the mottled circles which usually decorate its surface. I fancied that I detected waves sweeping its face. Might there be a glistening sea there onto which brave souls could venture out in ships?

"What is that?"

Dabir's question interrupted my imaginings. He pointed off to our right. A vast glow rose up from the sand somewhere to our northeast.

"Is it a city?"

"I have no idea," Dabir admitted. "It might be something useful. We should go see."

"What if it's something dangerous?"

"It might well be," Dabir acknowledged, but did not leave off

trotting down the side of the dune toward the glow.

I sighed inwardly and followed him. The light source did not prove to be as close as it first had seemed. Down we went, and up, and down and up again, and still the light remained mysterious and distant.

"Is it a mirage?"

"Mirages do not occur at night," Dabir said.

"Maybe they do here," I replied. He grunted, which might have been a yield to my point.

A half hour or more we walked before finally reaching the crest of a high, rippled dune and looking down upon a shining mystery.

All the sand had been cleared from a vast swath of the desert that stretched on for miles, exposing black bedrock. Set into that bedrock were countless thousands of twinkling lights.

"They look like the stars," I said.

"It is a map," Dabir said softly. "Someone has made a map of the stars. But it is backwards. See, there is the Coffin, and the Mourners. But Alioth is to the left of Mizar."

While I do not know the names of all the stars, I know many of the constellations, and I saw that Dabir was right.

"Who would go to all this trouble," I asked, "and set it up the wrong way?"

"And to what purpose?" Dabir asked. Doubtless he did not expect an answer from me. "Notice that some of the flickers

burn more brightly than others, just as real stars.

"Magic," I said.

Dabir crouched. "I would like a closer look."

"I do not recommend it. We cannot delay—we must find a way to stop Firouz."

"I thought you were the one who doubted there was a way out. If we are trapped, where lies the harm in looking?"

"I thought you were the one who said we could escape from here."

"Well, here is a marvel on our journey. We should stop to investigate, or we shall ever regret it."

"You said something like that before we walked through those doors."

"Asim, you told me not an hour ago that you were glad for the sight of these heavens."

"That does not negate my point! It is possible for things to get worse."

"Man"—an immense voice rang out of the stillness behind us—"what do you here?"

I whirled, hand to my sword, an oath on my lips.

If you're working with a team of heroes, be it two or three or more, one way to show that they are stronger together than apart is to show how they function while separated. Fritz Leiber does this to great effect in one of the very best entries in the Fahfrd and Gray Mouser cycle, "Lean Times in Lankhmar." In it, Fafhrd and the Mouser have a falling out, the former becoming acolyte to a priest of a minor god, the other a henchman for a local thug. Leiber doesn't bother showing us what temporarily ruins the relationship—indeed, he suggests several possibilities—but we see both characters acting in ways contrary to their more heroic standard until the inevitable, and hilarious, conclusion where they join forces once more.

Yes, team heroes can function apart, but usually not as effectively. Together, they are a greater hero than the sum of their attributes. The magic happens when they stand side-to-side or back-to-back; that's when the dialogue crackles, the foes fall, and the wrongs are righted.

I will end with one of my very favorite quotes about heroism, from Edison Marshall's foreword to his novel of Heracles, *Earth Giant*. Edison writes, "I feel mystically about heroes, whether Heracles, Arthur, Roland, Ragnar Lothbrok the great Viking, Siegfried, Captain John Smith, John Paul Jones, and some living in the last century or even alive today. It seems to me that the Gods love them, that Olympian lightning plays about their heads, that Chance suspends her dull laws when one of the breed comes nigh, that Fate will meet them more than halfway, that event in ratio to their own greatness is their daily fare as long as their heroism lives."

To that I would only add that, in the case of a pair of heroes, these things will be true so long as the two stand as one.

Monsters—Giving the Devils their Due

C. L. WERNER

What is it that really sets fantasy apart from mere historical fiction? Certainly you could argue it is the exotic lands and strange cultures, the arcane technology and mystic sorcery; however for me, the real magic in a fantasy story lies in its monsters. Strange beasts from the realm of nightmare, abhorrent creatures from the darkest pits of the psyche, demons drawn from the blackest reaches of the soul—these are the elements that tell the reader in no uncertain terms that he must leave his preconceptions at the door. The rules have changed. Anything can happen now. The monsters will make it so.

A well conceived monster can propel any story from the mundane into the mysterious. Some of the best examples of monster stories are those that begin by masquerading as something else, deceiving the reader that they will encounter only a normal western yarn or pot-boiled detective chronicle until the fantastic rears its ghastly head (if it even has a head, that is). The very normalcy of the surroundings goes far in such stories to magnify the monster's weird predilections and outré habits, increasing the menace it poses by heightening the wrongness of its very presence in a commonplace backdrop.

Unfortunately for the writer of fantasy tales, he cannot use his setting as a commonplace backdrop to heighten the malignance of his monsters. Whether set upon some imaginary world or placed within some forgotten corner of our own past, the stage is already far from what most readers would consider normal. The backdrop itself is something fantastical and new, a place of eldritch cultures and strange customs, archaic technologies and ancient cities. In such surroundings, where almost everything has a hint of the exotic about it, the poor old monster runs the risk of getting lost in the shuffle, just one more bizarre trapping attached to the story's background.

Reading fantasy fiction, it is quite easy to find examples where the author has squandered his opportunities and employed his monsters in just such a fashion. He takes no pains to make the beast stand out, treating it as casually as he would an old Paint standing beside a hitching post in Tombstone or a milk wagon trundling its way down a murky Chicago street. No special effort is made to breathe life—or menace—into the monster. Often such ill-treated beasts are introduced on one page and dispatched by the hero before the bottom of the next page.

> *The four orcs came rushing out from the trees, snarling harsh war cries, brandishing their swords overhead. Charging toward Ormgrim's mercenaries, the monsters were soon thrusting their blades at the armored men.*
>
> *"Hold fast!" the hulking barbarian roared to his men. He parried the blade of one orc with his buckler, then drove his axe into the skull of a second.*
>
> *"These beasts bleed!" Ormgrim bellowed. "And if they bleed, then they can die!"*

The poor orcs assaulting Ormgrim's sellswords don't have much going for them. They rush out of the trees, howling and shouting, waving their swords overhead, but nothing is really done to evoke any sense of the horrific. Our hero Ormgrim certainly reacts to them, but he doesn't seem particularly frightened. Indeed, it is just another day of carnage for the barbarian, of no more importance, consequence or uniqueness than an ordinary tavern brawl.

Such a casual approach to your monsters can work if they are not meant to be anything but a momentary, inconsequential blip on the hero's quest (though you should at least take a moment to describe in what way an orc is different from a perfectly normal human bandit or what separates your reptilian stalk-hound from a common wolf). However it is often the case where an author will unveil a swiftly executed combat such as the one above with little emotional involvement on the part of its participants and certainly not enough information to engage the reader's sensibilities, yet in the next paragraph he has the supporting cast toasting the hero on some grand accomplishment, feting him like the new lord of the land. Perhaps your preferences are different, but if a hero doesn't have any trouble (or at least some emotional misgivings) when he confronts the monster, then there's hardly anything there to celebrate.

As Lord Iskander approached the ruins, a dark shape loomed out of the shadows. The gleam of metal was in its hand, a broad-bladed curved sword, its cutting edge notched and serrated like the fangs of a wolf. Iskander caught the gleam of red eyes in the firelight reflecting from the blade, the suggestion of a broad ape-like snout squashed into a black-skinned face above a massive fanged jaw. The shape before him snarled.

"Tell your master I am here," Iskander demanded, his words conveying more courage than he felt. The creature before him snarled again, but turned, loping back into the ruins and toward the firelight. Iskander waited a moment, taking a deep

breath, steeling his nerves, then followed in
the path of the retreating orc.

In this second example, the perfidious Lord Iskander, obviously up to no good, has a slightly less hostile encounter with his orc than Ormgrim. However, the effect is much more dramatic and menacing. Through the prism of Iskander's eyes, we experience the intimidating presence of this slavering brute. The orc is described in his feral, savage appearance and nature, presenting the reader with a bit more vivid image of exactly how this creature is different from a man. In those differences, there lies the uncertainty of the unknown. We don't know exactly what is going on in this creature's primitive mind, and so we are compelled to rely upon Iskander's reactions as we form our own.

The menace of a monster lies as much in how the characters react to it as the amount of murder and havoc it can commit. Even the boldest hero should feel a twinge of doubt, perhaps even fear, when he faces the inhuman and otherworldly. He might not express it outwardly, but if we are given the impression that the hero himself is concerned about coming up against the monster, then we will be too. Like any good gunfighter in the Old West, a monster is only as intimidating as its reputation and the fear it provokes in those who confront it.

On the subject of reputation and fear, there is always the risk of selling your beast short when it comes to the inevitable battle with the hero. A great deal of well-crafted build-up can be simply wasted if your hero defeats the monster too easily or too quickly (unless, of course, that is the entire point). The struggle should be an epic contest between man and monster, don't squander the drama with a few sword swings and a quick one-liner. Play out the fight, choreograph it carefully and above all, push the hero to his limits. You should almost approach such scenes with a cinematic eye, relishing every moment of tension and drama, for what can be more dramatic than the destruction of some great and mighty monster?

Wolf steadied himself and advanced upon the sleeping god, his sword tensed to cleave the ophidian head from the scaly body. The German was certain that here was the very embodiment of the Enemy. Could a Christian encounter the Archfiend and fly from his presence, betraying the faith he espoused? For the knight there could be but one course of action.

As Wolf's blade of Rhineland steel sang through the air, the great serpent's yellow eyes rolled back into life, immediately seeing the arc of gleaming death descending upon its neck. With a loud hiss, the serpent darted backward. In doing so, though it avoided the German's death blow, the sword bit into the side of the monster's head, cleaving its left eye in twain and passing through the serpent's scaly lips. Black blood spurted from the wyrm's wound and sizzled as it struck the hot floor of the cavern.

Wolf stood his ground, roaring his defiance at the great wyrm as it reared back and rose to the very height of the cavern, its head dozens of feet above the knight. But Wolf had been emboldened by the sight of the wyrm's blood and the knowledge that what he thought a devil was in truth a beast of flesh and bone.

Quetzalcoatl hissed loudly, its sound like that of a red-hot blade being plunged into icy water. The great serpent spread its wings in a gesture of anger, the tips of the massive pinions striking either wall of the cathedral-like cavern. Wolf shuddered at the sight, rethinking the beast's mortality. Lit by the lava pools and highlighted by the shadows, it seemed as though the serpent had reared up from the Pit itself.

Like one of Jove's thunderbolts, the serpent's head plunged downward from its great height, the monster folding its wings against its sides once more as it hurtled at the little man who stood before it. But luck was with the knight and the serpent's fangs missed him, the reptile unable to compensate for its impaired vision. Before the wyrm could retreat from its attack, Wolf's sword bit deeply into its neck.

Blood slopped from Quetzalcoatl's neck in a gory waterfall as the monster reared upward. The hissing of the reptile had ceased and in its place there came a ghastly gurgle. Again Quetzalcoatl bared its scimitar-like fangs and dropped upon the knight. So swift was the assault that no creature could have avoided it. The fangs struck Wolf's chest, piercing his mail but sinking no deeper. The serpent found its curved fangs caught in the interlocking rings of steel, trapped fast by the unyielding metal.

The White Wyrm raised its head once more, taking with it the armored warrior hanging from its fangs. Even as the wyrm thrashed its head fiercely from side to side in a savage attempt to free itself, even as Wolf found himself bashed against wall and ceiling, the German's blade struck again and again at the monster's head, drinking deeply of the reptile's blood.

Will Wolf prevail against the serpentine monstrosity the people of Culuacan call Quetzalcoatl? Well, he's certainly making a good fight of it at least. Success and failure can take a back seat to a truly heroic struggle. If the obstacle to overcome is awesome enough, the reader won't feel cheated if the hero falls before it and such a bittersweet ending can leave a real impact when done properly, much more so than the comfortable satisfaction of having Perseus behead Medusa or Beowulf visit the death-blow upon Grendel's mother. Above all, win or lose, the encounter with this ferocious monstrosity should be something the reader will remember.

Something worth considering when writing about different monsters is getting inside their heads. Feel out what makes them tick. If your vampire acts like a normal person with normal thoughts, he'll lose a lot of his horrific potency. Distance him from rational thought, give him strange and inhuman desires (beyond the obvious lust for blood) and you'll have a much more frightening character. If you write about intelligent rodents, don't have the rats simply mirror the way we think. Take a cue from the instincts and habits of real rats and incorporate them into the mindset of your monster. This is a tact that has made my interpretation of the skaven in my *Warhammer* novels for the Black Library immensely popular, if a bit slimy and foul. If you are writing about a reptilian abomination from the dawn of time, then take a little extra effort to make it act like a reptile. Make it sensitive to heat and cold, play upon its primitive biology to create something that isn't simply an everyday domestic animal with a skin problem.

A lot of times, it is the small details that can really make your monsters stand out. Have a little extra thought about their habits and the mind which gives them motivation (however small and unreasoning that mind might be). If you can give the creature just a few extra details that set it beyond the norm, the effect can be profound. Often the more low-key and minor the detail, the more impressive its impact upon the reader.

The Taliosian and the remaining Isicarite, a hulking brute named Kormaz, were watching one of the snake-creatures which had not fled with its comrades. The monster was striking at a fallen torch, hacking at the flame with its copper sword. Grenulf looked at the hacked and mutilated bodies of the fallen Isicarites and understood. The creatures were blind, born into a world of eternal darkness. Blind, yet they could sense heat and warmth, sense it and strike at it, attacking dead flesh time and again until all warmth had bled from the corpse.

Even when presenting a monster that is benevolent, exploiting similar tactics can create a disturbing, eerie atmosphere of wrongness about the creature. When the hero treats with any fantastic being, there should be at least some element of anxiety present, a hint that all is not quite right in the world. In my short story "Bodyguard of the Dead" (*Demons*, Rogue Blades Entertainment, 2010), the mummified priest Kambei-kai, while a force of good in the story, is still presented as a thing of horror. A shriveled *sokushinbutsu*, the priest is unable to speak and communicates by writing messages which his monkish attendant reads aloud for him. Unable to drink or eat, the mummy indulges in a cup of tea by inhaling the steam. All in all, he's a sinister sort of character, yet one who is sided with the powers of good against the forces of darkness. All of the horrific trappings add to the mystery and mysticism of Kambei-kai and help to set him in stark contrast to the far cruder, more physical malevolence of his adversary, the oni Ushitora.

It is also worth considering that a monster can be especially crafted to highlight the character of your hero, a Hyde to his Jekyll as it were. If your hero is a pious Crusader, what could be more of a test of his character than some Satanic demon conjured up from the pits of

Hell? Maybe your hero is a world-weary hunter who is forced to reluctantly accept the duty of dispatching a marauding griffon. How would this tired-old hunter react to being impressed into such service? Would he accept the labor as an honor or as an ordeal? Would he sympathize with the farmers and peasants threatened by the beast, or would his sympathies lie with the predatory griffon—a creature he might have more in common with than his fellow man? If your hero is a knightly lord whose castle and family were destroyed by a dragon, how might he react to such a monster? Would he cast aside all thoughts of honor and chivalry in his lust for vengeance? Would he become an obsessed sociopath, not caring how many warriors he leads to destruction or how many innocents perish so long as he can have his revenge?

A monster used in such fashion becomes a mirror to reflect the quality of the hero, cutting deep into his psyche to expose the core of his beliefs and ideals. In these cases, the monster's claws and fangs might be less of a threat to the hero than what the beast itself represents to him.

There is, of course, a far different approach to monsters that serves equally well when executed skillfully. We've discussed describing the beasts, getting inside their heads, displaying their unusual habits. Now, we'll talk about throwing all of that out the window. If you don't want your monster to stand out in the light and bellow its challenge to the sky, then the other track is to keep the thing concealed in the shadows.

Less is more when using your monster in this fashion. Fleeting glimpses, the suggestion of a few horrific details of a monstrous physiognomy, the awful carnage of the monster's depredations, these are the tools that will serve you when you want to keep the beast obscure. To be sure, it is even more important to have the characters react appropriately and more than ever your hero can't be immune to feeling at least some level of fear and displaying it for the reader's benefit. The crawling malignity of the unknown is probably the most potent weapon in a writer's arsenal when evoking uneasiness in his audience, but it is also one of the hardest to sustain. It takes a careful hand to conceal the details from his readers without causing them to feel cheated. The payoff, however, is certainly worth the risk.

> *Last of all, Granddad would tell us about the Horror. No one ever did give it a name or call it anything outside of "the Horror." There's an old belief that evil things notice when you talk about them, especially if you speak their name. I suppose that tradition still lingers on. Here in New York, there's an expression: "You must have been talking about me because my ears are burning." Well, it was the same sort of thing back then, except it wasn't regarded flippantly at all. Like I say, it was never called anything more than "the Horror."*

Treat your monsters well, and they will serve you well. After all the pains you take crafting your plot, planning out the character of your dashing hero and despicable villain, it only makes sense to put a little extra effort into the unnatural fiends which stand between the hero and his goal. A well-realized monster is something that will stick in a reader's mind long after the story is done. The more magnificent your monster is in its horror, the more magnificent your hero will look when he finally brings about the beast's downfall.

Npcs are People Too

JENNIFER BROZEK

Writing fiction is more than just telling a story. It is building a world for the reader to enjoy, dream about, and to get lost in. This means building a framework that can support your story. One of the most important bits of the framework is the NPCs—the Non-Player Characters. These are the extras on the scene of a movie. These are the people your heroes will need to interact with for any number of reasons.

WHY IS AN NPC IMPORTANT?

Most often, an NPC in a scene is there to give the main character (thus, the reader) information about the story in question. This information can be used to drive the character or the plot forward, to tell the reader about the world, or to tell the reader something about the main characters or heroes of the piece.

The NPC helps to fill out the world in other ways as well. They can be used to demonstrate the tone of a scene, fill out the setting, and to let the reader see the world through more than just the main characters' eyes. In my piece, "The Prince of Artemis V" (*Stalking the Wild Hare*, Walkabout Publishing, 2010) I write:

> *"They all look at me like she's already been Taken," Hart heard his mother say. He could imagine the distressed flush of*

Jennifer Brozek

109

his mother's face. "We've got to do something."

"The Company doesn't give a damn what happens to us. As long as the purpuran flowers are harvested and the royal dye is made, they don't care." In his mind's eye, Hart could see his father's drawn face and strength failing in his old man's body.

The father isn't important to the story. He is an NPC. However, with his words to his wife, I am able to express that the situation is not a new one and there is no help coming. I did not have to say any of this specifically. It is merely part of the world that Hart and Hart's parents live in. This scene between the NPCs, overheard by the hero, tells the hero just how bad the situation is getting on an emotional level.

To push the example further, your NPC is frequently a catalyst for the hero to do the right thing. Later, in "The Prince of Artemis V" I write:

Saneri took the small smile as a sign of encouragement. "I love you, Hart. You're the one I can depend on. You always have been." She paused, took a breath and then forged onward, "That's why I need you to protect your sister."

"Because you and Dad can't."

She looked away and nodded, but not before he saw the flinch of pain on her face. "Yes. You're closer to her. She idolizes you. You...I—I think you're her only hope."

Now that the truth was out between them—almost all of it anyway—Hart nodded at her, feeling better. He was Lanteri's only hope. He knew it. He had always known it. "Don't worry, Mom. I'll

protect her. I promise." The look of
gratitude on his mother's face was painful
but he smiled at it. "I know what to do."

Hart's mother, the NPC, comes out and asks Hart to be the hero that he is. When his mother admits she doesn't know what to do, it puts the weight of responsibility on Hart and he needs to step up to his role in the story or deny it. Here, he accepts his role as hero. It doesn't hurt that he is emotionally invested in both his NPC mother and NPC sister.

The presence of NPCs, in a generic sense, can also indicate the transition of tone in a story; the gathering of zombies outside the farmhouse where the heroes are hiding, the presence of two guards outside of a hospital room, the crowd of teenagers waiting for the show to start. All of these set the tone of the scene and all of them convey a message. In my short story, "M.O.V.E." (*No Man's Land*, Dark Quest Books, 2011) I write:

> *The faceless security personnel in their*
> *combat helmets did not relax their guard*
> *as they pulled the cadets from the Epiet's*
> *vessel. The girls saw that security was*
> *covering the male Epiet who was still*
> *down or unconscious while the female*
> *Epiet was dragged from the vessel and*
> *dropped to the floor next to her*
> *companion. They all stood there, cadets*
> *with their hands raised, covered by two*
> *security men while a third reported the*
> *situation.*
> *"Your sponsors, Guardsmen Haber and*
> *Rillion, are on their way, Cadets. I hope*
> *you have a good explanation for what*
> *happened here," the security officer said as*
> *he got off the com-unit.*

Jennifer Brozek

111

"We do, sir. It's one for the books,"
Natara said.
"I'll bet. At ease."
Soolee and Natara dropped into a
semi-formal parade rest stance.

The way the NPCs hold weapons on the heroes of the story (Soolee, Natara) tells you about the tenseness of the situation. The cadets are harmless but the situation they are in is not. Then, as the NPC security officer speaks to the cadets, the tension of the situation is diffused, moving from danger to waiting and transitioning to the next scene. Finally, the causal way the security guard answers the cadets speaks of the man's comfort with authority and cadets. You can almost see the security officer sizing up the heroes, determining that they have been through something interesting but that they are not the threat here.

Whereas, earlier in the story, the female Epiet was the threat to the cadets and could see that the cadets were a threat to her as shown in:

For one instant, Natara was sure someone else was in the room with Soolee. In the next, she was positive she was being paranoid. Her next step told her that her gut instinct had been correct.

Another smaller Epiet was in the corner of the room with a weapon pointed at Soolee while looking at the door. The Epiet opened its mouth to speak but Natara did not hesitate. She opened fire on the alien. The first shot missed, hitting the cabinet next to the Epiet's shoulder. The second shot hit her in the chest. The Epiet got off one shot that grazed Natara's left arm. Natara yelped in pain and fired again. She struck the Epiet in the chest again. This time, the Epiet dropped its weapon and slumped to the floor. As its

*last living act, the Epiet reached over and
twisted something on its belt. The light in
the small ship blinked from the standard
white to an ominous yellow.*

This interaction with the NPC spurred the hero to
react, rather than act, telling the reader that the hero had
good instincts, was a good shot and did not hesitate to
protect a comrade in arms. It also ratcheted up the tension
of the scene with the NPC activating something to
become a new obstacle for the heroes.

One of the most important things an NPC can do is tell
you something about the main character—hero or
villain—of the piece. In my story, "Iron Achilles Heel"
(*The New Hero II*, Stone Skin Press, 2013) I write:

> *"There's something up ahead."*
> *Joseph was back within Eric and he
> could feel the Sheriff's lingering pain on
> the edges of his senses. He pushed it away
> and concentrated on the moving thing in
> his path. His heart sank as he got closer. It
> was a downed horse. A live one, in pain.*
> *With his pistol drawn, he approached,
> looking all around. The horse groaned
> loud when it saw Eric. Its eyes begged him
> to stop the pain. To help it, somehow.
> There was a touch of a squeal in its next,
> more urgent groan and Eric could see its
> front foreleg was broken. "That bastard
> left you to suffer."*
> *"No. I think he left her here as a way to
> tell how close you were getting."*
> *Joseph was right; Eric knew it and did
> not need to question his spirit mentor's
> comment. The choice was to either
> immediately end the horse's suffering with*

a bullet in the brain or to cause more pain
and a slower death with a cut throat.
  "What will you do?"
  "I don't know. What would you do?"
  "This is your hunt. Your choice."
Joseph paused and added, "Choose with
your heart."
  "Are you testing me again? Because if
you are, it's starting to irritate me."
  "What will you do?" Joseph asked
again.
  "The right thing." With that, he put his
pistol to the suffering horse's head and told
the outlaw exactly where he was...also told
him the kind of man who was tracking him.

The NPC in this case was the horse in pain. The NPC
was used to show the reader something about the main
villain and the main hero—one is willing to make others
suffer and the other is willing to give up his advantage to
stop that suffering. The horse in pain is an NPC that is
used to also touch the heartstrings of the reader and to
encourage them to think, 'You bastard!' at the bad guy. It
is an emotional play that is also memorable. Then, the
hero makes the choice to end the suffering as quickly as
possible and to harden his heart against pleas for mercy.
This is the moment in the story when the 'shit gets real.'

There are a number of things that an NPC is used for
but, in the end, the NPC is a tool for the author to show
the reader something, tell the main character something,
to set the scene and to set the tone for what is to come.

HOW DO YOU MAKE AN NPC REAL?

One of the hardest things in a story is to make an NPC
real in a way that allows the reader to care, in some small
way, about them. They are not just there to info-dump. To
make your writing that much better, you must treat every

NPC as if they could suddenly take over the story or become, at the very least, a secondary character. This means they have lives just like the main characters. There is more to them in the back of your mind than them being scenery that bleeds. For example, in my story, "Iron Achilles Heel" I write:

With time to kill, Eric inspected what was left of the Marlin camp. Daniel had done a good job of ransacking it. There was nothing useful left. Then he saw a glimmer of light from Jeb's left hand. Upon removal and some squinting in the scant starlight, Eric discovered that it was a wedding ring.

"Huh. I didn't know he was married."
He turned the ring over and around before reading, "With Love, Anne."

"Even outlaws find love," Joseph said. "You know you can use that as proof of your kill."

"My kill?"

"There's still a bounty on Jebadiah's head—dead or alive. That ring you just pocketed proves you deserve it."

Eric scowled, "No, it doesn't. I didn't have anything to do with Jeb's death. I'm not a murderer."

"Ah, but you are."

"No." He shook his head, "You spirit-ride me. You do the killing."

"While you get the reward and accolades?"

Eric swung his head from side to side. He wasn't hearing Joseph's voice in his head. That meant the Sheriff was around but, for some reason, the spirit stayed hidden. He wanted to face his accuser, but suppressed his growing anger at the man's accusations. "That's not why I do this."

"Then why'd you take the ring?"
Eric's voice was quiet. "Even an
outlaw's wife deserves to know her
husband's dead and who really killed him."
Joseph did not respond. He remained
quiet until they were well on their way to
finding Daniel Marlin.

In this particular case, the NPC was a dead outlaw. When Eric finds the ring, he realizes that the outlaw had a life beyond killing. This touches him and makes him realize that the wife needs to know that her husband is dead. Joseph, the other main character, uses this act to press home a fact that Eric has been denying: that he is as much of a killer as the spirit he occasionally hosts.

When I write a story, a vignette or any other fiction that involves main characters and NPCs, I always have a series of five questions I have answered in the back of my head about them. If I know the NPC is going to be a recurring character, I add five more questions and I keep that information in a file.

My five questions are:

+ **What does this person do for a living?** I ask this question because, based on the time and day of the week, I know what they are basically wearing and how they should be acting. And if they are in a professional capacity, are they subservient or authoritarian?
+ **What does this person do for fun?** This tells me about their hobbies—where I would find them, if they would have sports gear on them or books or tickets. Also, if they happen to wear a particular band, sports team or political slogan. Based on what they see of the main character, this may color their reaction to them.
+ **Are they married or single?** This is important because it gives people a basis for personal interactions with the main character—asexual,

hound dog, protective of family—all important pieces of information for social interaction.

✦ **Do they have any physical or noticeable quirks?** This can be anything from a stutter to a limp to a penchant for loud clothing. They may be deaf or they may tap their fingers on everything. No person is perfect and all people are different. This is something to give this NPC a little bit of specialness.

✦ **What do they love/hate?** This last question really depends on my mood and the type of story I'm telling. Love or hate, everyone has a strong emotion toward something—love of kittens, hatred of roses, love of blonds, hatred of gum chewers. Again, while this may not come into play in the scene, it is there in the back of my mind to use as needed.

For recurring NPCs, my additional five questions are:

✦ **Do they own pets?** The owning of pets tells me a lot about the NPC. Do they care enough to have a pet? Do they care for it? Are they covered in pet hair? Do they like non-traditional pets? If they don't have a pet, why not?

✦ **Do they have a code of ethics?** A code of ethics is an important thing in a recurring NPC. It will affect how they treat the main character or the situation at hand. How do they deal with bribes? Do they stay bought? Are they strict on following the law? All of these things will affect the story you are telling.

✦ **Are they rich, middle class, or poor?** This will tell you something about where they live and what they eat. Do they need to sacrifice to get luxuries or do they have diamonds dripping off their wrists?

✦ **Generous or tight-fisted?** Will they give the shirt off their back to help a stranger in need or will they hoard that quarter even though they have all the money they need? This affects how they speak—willing to give information or needing to be bought—and how they will interact in a conversation with your main character.

✦ **What's their favorite color?** This may seem like a silly question but, for me, it gives me a lot to go on subconsciously. Red = aggressive, lusty. Orange = outgoing and strange. Things like that.

It does not matter what your five or ten questions are, just that you have them and that you use them. When you write your story with the NPC on scene or being talked about, having these questions answered for yourself will give you the upper hand to writing a more realistic NPC and setting for your heroes to walk through.

As an aside, I have all of these questions already answered for my main characters and more so. A fully fleshed out main character is paramount to a story. Even if you never use the fact that your main character loves the color orange and collects My Little Ponies® while loathing the very sight of cut flowers, you have those quirks in your subconscious and can use them to explain away why they hated the picture of flowers in a vase or why they noticed the orange car.

HINTS, TRICKS, AND TIPS

No author works in a vacuum—at least, not the good ones. To know how NPCs should act to be real, look around you to see how the NPCs in your life act. Thus, I have a series of activities to use to allow your NPCs to come to life in a way that makes them realistic while not running away with the scene.

✦ **Make a list.** Make a list of people you interact with but do not really talk to on a day-to-day basis. These people can include baristas, bus drivers, mailmen, couriers, taxi drivers, shopkeepers, grocery store cashiers and baggers—the list goes on. Think about each of these people and what you know about them even if you haven't really spoken to them. The courier obviously works out based on his physique. The barista is in school based on the book she reads in her down time. The bagger had a bad fall based on her limp and it was probably due to skiing based on the ski tag dangling from her jacket. When you sit and think about it, your subconscious picks up on a lot of clues you are not consciously aware of. You know more about the people around you than you think you do. These people are the NPCs in your life. You can take this experience and use it in your writing.

✦ **NPC note cards are your friend.** When I am writing a game or a story and I need a lot of NPCs I need to keep distinct and separate, I use my NPC note cards. This is a stack of note cards with a bunch of readymade NPCs on them. Each of my note cards has a name, gender, occupation, basic description and answers to the first five questions listed above. I make these note cards based on the NPCs in my life—who I live near, who I interact with, who I observe and, occasionally, random people on the street who catch my eye.

Yes, I break the rule about not using friends and family but I rarely, if ever, link a real name with a real background on an NPC card. Frequently, I will also change the gender of the person I am basing the NPC on. The biggest trick to using people you know as NPCs is to take one or two aspects of that person and exaggerate them to the point of obfuscation. This is part of writing what (or who, in this case) you know.

✦ **Eavesdrop in a public place.** Sometimes it is hard to come up with a readymade personality on the fly. Even when basing NPCs on people you know, you need extra inspiration. The best and easiest way to do this is to go to a public place like a mall, coffee shop, or any other place where people congregate—airports, subway stations or the DMV—and eavesdrop. Listen to whom they talk to and how. Watch how the ticket taker deals with the public or the teenage girl works the counter. Does she smile or frown? Listen to how people talk to each other. It certainly isn't in formal language. Half the time, conversations between people, even strangers, is in a kind of verbal shorthand. Watch how they speak with gestures as much as they do with language. You can take all of that and use it in your writing. It is just one more way of making your NPCs as real as possible.

Also, as a side note, eavesdropping on conversations can give you all sorts of interesting ideas for stories. And overheard secret or misunderstood comment can blossom into the best storylines that you would never have thought up on your own. There is no shame in public eavesdropping. After all, these are real people with 'stranger than fiction' lives. The only thing you may have to do is tone down the weirdness on what you overhear. My editors would not let me use a lot of what I actually overhear because it is too outrageous to believe. Real life doesn't have to make sense but your fiction does.

In the end, your NPCs can be your most important asset to help tell your story. They can impart information to the reader, move your story along, help show important aspects of the main character that you might not otherwise be able to show, can help describe what is going on around the main characters and set the tone for the scene. NPCs are people, too, and worthy of your consideration.

Tropes of the Trade

ARI MARMELL

Let's talk tropes.

If you do any reading or socializing in groups of writers—or even die-hard readers—you've heard people refer to "tropes." These are, in the most basic terms, common concepts of the genre. The "Chosen One," prophesied to bring down an ancient evil, is a trope. The all-powerful object that everyone's after, such as the One Ring—what Hitchcock referred to as the McGuffin—is a trope. The standard array of fantasy races—human, elf, dwarf, hobbit/halfling—popularized by Tolkien and then *Dungeons & Dragons®* is a trope. Tropes can be plot points, setting details, basic descriptions, what have you.

"But Ari," you might say, "isn't that just another word for 'cliché'? Don't you want to try to be original and avoid those?"

To which I might respond, "I can't hear you. You're talking to a book, you turkey."

But if I *could* hear you, what I might say is this:

Originality is great—as a *tool* for writing good stories and creating compelling characters, or as a *byproduct* thereof. It should never be your *goal*; your goals should be, well, writing a good story and creating compelling characters.

And for that, tropes are just another tool in the writer's toolkit. Like any tool, you want to avoid them when they aren't right for the job, but you absolutely want to make full use of them when they *are*.

Ari Marmell

121

They're the right tool for the job a surprising amount of the time.

(For purposes of this essay, I'm going to gloss over one of the single most important traits of tropes in fantasy, which is, quite simply, that lots of people *like* them. Just as audiences often gravitate toward food that's similar to what they already like, or TV shows similar to the ones they already watch, many people find delight— or at least comfort—in novels that have lots of traits in common with those they've already read. There's a reason that many tropes *are* tropes, and it's because people enjoy seeing them. It's why so many heroes follow common archetypes: the valorous knight, the brooding loner, the farm boy with a destiny. It's why so many books contain the same basic races, or are clearly based on Medieval Europe when there are so many other fascinating cultures to explore or create. But while this is a vital point to remember, and one of the best reasons not to eschew the use of tropes, this knowledge doesn't help you understand when, how, or why to use said tropes in your writing. Thus, it's an interesting but not particularly useful observation for our purposes.)

TROPES AS SHORTHAND

"What's your name, child?" asked the voice from behind.

"T-Tyannon, my lord."

"Tyannon." The name rolled around in the speaker's mouth, as though tasting it for imperfections. "And why am I speaking to the back of your head, Tyannon?"

"B-because I'm f-facing the other way, my lord?"

Most of the captives, and indeed several of the guards, gasped in disbelief, and the young woman tensed in expectation of a sudden blow. After a moment of silence, however, a soft chuckle was the only response.

Then, "Turn around, Tyannon."

Her shoulders slumping, as if she'd consigned herself to whatever fate the gods might hold in store, she obeyed.

The figure looming before her came straight from one of the fairy tales she read to Jass every night—one of the darker ones. Shorter than his ogre minions, he nonetheless loomed over her, filling the entirety of her vision. A demonic suit of armor concealed his body, head to toe: midnight black steel, with thick plates of bone that gleamed unnaturally white in the orange glow of the lanterns. From small spines of bone on his shoulders hung a heavy cloak of royal purple, a coincidental match to the regent's banner on the fields outside. The flickering lanterns sent his shadow dancing across the walls, as though guided by some mad puppeteer. Atop it all, a helm of bone, a skull bound in iron bands. Nothing human showed through the grim façade, no soul peered from the gaping black holes in the mask.

With a desperate surge of will, the young woman pulled her gaze away from the hideous mask, glancing downward instead. Her eyes fixed momentarily on the chain about his neck. It dipped down beneath the bone-covered breastplate, linked perhaps to some pendant or amulet she couldn't see. Her eyes traveled lower still, to the large double-bladed axe upon which his gauntlet rested. It stood upright, butt of the handle upon the ground. The blade was adorned with minuscule engravings—abstract shapes that gave the impression, though not the detail, of thousands of figures engaged in the cruelest, most brutal acts of war. Tyannon whimpered quietly as she saw that there were worse things to stare at than the blackened eye sockets of the helm. Things like that axe, and the figures engraved upon it, figures that seemed almost to move on their own, independent from the dancing torchlight . . .

(from *The Conqueror's Shadow*,
prologue, Spectra, 2009)

The dark-armored evil warlord would certainly qualify as a trope, if ever there was one. As soon as the reader sees this, he or she knows, to an extent, what to expect. It's been drummed into the audience for years. Darth Vader; Lord Soth; the Nazgûl, more or less; Sauron himself, if we're talking about the opening of *The Fellowship of the Ring* movie; Doctor Doom, from Marvel Comics.

And, in my own novel, Corvis Rebaine. When we first meet Corvis, he's in full-on warlord mode, at the height of his power as the "Terror of the East." And we meet him, not really as a human being, but as an imposing suit of black armor, complete with spines of bone and a skull-shaped helm. It's clearly intended to be intimidating more than to actually function in combat. (Any swordsman will tell you that spines on armor just help guide weapons in.) But while that armor sends a message to the people he's conquering—"Be afraid"—the message it sends to the reader is "You already know, in part, who and what this guy is."

It's that last bit that we're focusing on here. That description does more than tell the reader what Corvis looks like; because it builds on a common trope, it tells the reader a great deal about his personality and even his goals in a very brief span of time. It's not enough, by itself; relying on tropes without plot/character development to back them up, is where you drift into the realm of cliché. (More on that in a bit.) But it's a useful start.

Essentially, I've used the "villainous black knight" trope as a shorthand language to convey far more information than the description alone. You'll find, I think, that tropes are used this way more often than almost any other; as a secondary language—the "body language" of written text, if you will—to add a layer of meaning that the words themselves don't necessarily carry.

Those heroic archetypes I mentioned above? They all serve this purpose. The archetypes aren't enough, in and of themselves; you have to expand on them, delve into them. But by establishing what sort of hero you're writing about, you immediately give the reader a basis from which to start building their picture of the character—and to an extent, the entire story.

That said, the shorthand language of tropes isn't limited to individual characters; it can be used to tell the reader about the world, or even the purpose of a story. If a tale refers to nobles as kings, queens, dukes, barons, etc.; if it involves fortified castles, or a monolithic Church; if it involves knights in armor on heavy warhorses; then it's most likely based on Medieval Europe, and this, in turn, often tells the reader what *other* societal details to expect. The presence of armored knights doesn't *require* the existence of a traditional feudal monarchy; a monolithic religious institution doesn't *have* to be modeled on the Roman Catholic Church. But while such associations aren't *automatic*, they're certainly more common than not.

Lots of stories—*Star Wars* being perhaps the most famous example—deliberately follow the model of Joseph Campbell's "monomyth" (also known as the "Hero's Journey"). Many stories follow this archetype to a greater or lesser extent, but those that do so overtly and deliberately are making use of well established tropes in

Ari Marmell

their structure. Heck, their structure arguably *is* a trope unto itself. As soon as you start seeing these tropes appear—"the call to adventure," "refusal of the call," "supernatural aid," and so forth (largely in that order)— then the author has already told you, at least in very broad terms, what sort of tale to expect and what sort of emotions he or she is trying to evoke.

TROPES AS DECEPTION

He wasn't an especially conspicuous figure, not like in his younger days. He was taller than average—taller than most of the men in the village, certainly. In his prime, he'd been mountainous, his body covered with layers of rock-solid muscle; even Xavier, Renfro's large son, was a delicate flower compared to what this man once had been.

Middle age stole that from him, though a combination of strict exercise and natural inclination saved him from going to fat, as so many former men of war inevitably did. He was, in fact, quite wiry now, slender to the point of gaunt. His face was one of edges and angles, striking without being handsome, and the gaze of his green eyes piercing. Hair once brown had greyed; it hung just past his neck, giving him a vaguely feral demeanor. Even now he could do the work of a man half his age, but he wasn't what he used to be.

And his back still hurt.

"Daddy, Daddy!"

The grin that blossomed across his face washed away the pain in his back. Quickly he knelt down, catching the wiggling brown-haired flurry that flung itself into

his arms. Standing straight, he cradled the
child to his breast, laughing.
(from *The Conqueror's Shadow*,
chapter one, Spectra, 2009)

On the other hand, that exact same shorthand can be used to *mislead*, rather than *inform*, in order to hammer home a point or introduce a "swerve" in the story. The above description doesn't particularly stand out; it's just an average fellow (albeit one who was quite dangerous in his youth), not uncommon in this sort of fantasy setting.

It's *also* the same character described in the previous excerpt, albeit quite some time later—a sharp contrast that works, in part, because of the images and associations that come with the "black knight" trope.

While Corvis is clearly a villain in the first excerpt, he's actually the *protagonist* for most of the book. By using a standard trope to hammer home who/what Corvis was seventeen years ago, it makes the transformation into who he is "now" that much more dramatic; the line of demarcation between who he is and who he was that much sharper. If the reader didn't already have a strong image of Corvis Rebaine as "warlord/black knight," there wouldn't be nearly as much punch to seeing him, only a chapter later, as "aging family man."

In Simon R. Green's *Blue Moon Rising*, he begins with the protagonist in a very traditional quest—to rescue a maiden from a dragon—in part as a contrast to the rest of the book, which abruptly turns in a very different direction. (The dragon is peaceful, and the princess is happier here than she was at home, just for starters.)

Just as you can use existing tropes to convey information to the reader, you can also use them to convey a deliberate false impression. Anyone who assumes that the earlier description of Corvis defines who he is for the entire book, for example, is going to find themselves making a quick about-face in the next chapter. It's a powerful way for writers to play with—and even

Ari Marmell

127

tweak—reader expectations. (And if that sounds manipulative, well, yeah. That's what writers *do*: Manipulate.) You don't want to out-and-out *lie* to readers (unless you're speaking from the point of view of an unreliable character or narrator, of course), but a trope can make the reader *think* they know what you're doing while you then build off of it in some other direction.

This technique can be applied to setting and other aspects of storytelling, but it works best when building characters. True heroism is more impressive when it comes from an unexpected source; this sort of "authorial slight-of-hand" allows you to surprise the reader, play with expectations, make a seemingly mundane or even good-for-nothing character into a genuine hero (or, of course, to prove a seemingly heroic character actually weak and cowardly). Nobody is at all surprised that Luke winds up leading the final attack on the Death Star, because by then, we expected heroics from him. The pivotal reappearance of the "scoundrel" Han Solo, however, has more of an emotional impact—or at least it did, back in the mists of time when the movie was new—precisely because it comes from a less overtly heroic source. Had Han not been played up as a selfish mercenary to that point, his later heroic actions wouldn't have carried nearly the same impact.

(And he shot first, damn it.)

TROPES AS GENRE

You know what else tropes are really good for? Firmly establishing yourself in the fantasy (or other) genre. In fact, one could argue that they're *essential*. What is genre, but the trappings and descriptive details of a story and setting? Certainly, in some genres, what matters is what happens in the story. If you're writing a romance novel, your story has to be focused on romance; if you're writing a mystery, your story must have unknown aspects to be investigated and twists to be revealed.

But fantasy? Science-fiction? These are genres defined, for the most part, by *details*. Does the story have magic? Is it set on a secondary world? Does it include monsters? (It's possible for the answers to these to be *no*, and for a story to still be fantasy; but if the answers to these are all *yes*, then the story, almost by definition, *must* be fantasy.) The trappings of the setting firmly cement the tale in the fantasy genre, and what are said trappings—in many cases—but the use of the genre's common tropes?

Of course, there's some disagreement, as there always will be in any non-scientific field. Heck, this book's own editor and I have been involved in a rather intense debate as to whether a certain story qualifies as "sword-and-sorcery," based on the actions and attitudes of the story's protagonist. (And we weren't on the same side of said debate, I should point out). But whether one believes in a stricter or looser definition, it's still the presence or absence of certain tropes on which one is likely basing the bulk of one's argument.

(One could argue as to whether or not it *matters* if a story fits perfectly into a given genre. Odds are, it really doesn't. But that's a different question entirely.)

TROPES AS SATIRE

Deliberately evoking fantasy tropes beyond what's strictly necessary for a story—sometimes to the point of cliché—can certainly be a sign of bad or amateurish writing, but it might also be a deliberate act on the part of the writer in order to create humor or to point out some absurdity in the genre. Peter David's *Sir Apropos of Nothing* series is, essentially, a parody of fantasy with a genuine story running through it. In the aforementioned Simon Green novel, both the characters and the narrator are able to squeeze a fair amount of wry humor out of the very traditional circumstances. In *The Goblin Corps* (Pyr Books, 2011), I sometimes deliberately emphasize the classic fantasy tropes—multi-racial adventuring parties, empires of good and evil, etc.—in order to more dramatically frame the actions and natures of the goblin races who, though evil, are the *protagonists* of the book.

Obviously, there are limits to how far you can go with this unless you're writing what is meant to be a comic story. An element of parody or satire can go over just fine as a spice; too much of it, though, and a book becomes impossible to take seriously. It's a fine line to walk.

ALTERING, TWEAKING, AND DISGUISING

Smoothly, two forms broke the surface of the water. The first was Urkran; his eye was stretched wide with shock, his breathing shallow, his formerly red skin a sickly shade of pale. Here and there, a few stubborn spots of blood clung to his limbs or his clothes. His weapons were gone, embedded in the mud, not that they'd have done him any good. He was too weak even to turn his head, much less raise a hand in defiance of the creature slowly murdering him.

The other form emerging from the heavy murk was his killer. Less than half the ogre's height, it appeared almost human. A face that didn't quite qualify as round—puffy, perhaps, was a better word—was topped by a matted mane of black hair, plastered to his scalp by the surrounding waters. His eyes were cold, piercing, and tinted with the faintest hint of crimson. His lips, fish-pale and thin, gaped open to reveal perfectly white and straight teeth.

The thing leaned over the ogre, those narrow lips a hairsbreadth from Urkran's ear. Placing his mouth against the ogre's cheek, it inhaled. Urkran moaned in revulsion as he felt the pores of his skin stretch wide, felt his own blood flow through the newly-opened gaps. He shuddered as the creature's tongue danced over his face, determined not to miss a single drop of the ogre's draining life.

(from *The Conqueror's Shadow*, chapter eight, Spectra, 2009)

Nor was Losalis finished. With a grunt he pivoted on a single foot. The snow slowed him, threatened to trip him up, yet he muscled his way through. The saber, yanked free, whistled around again as he completed his spin and cleaved cleanly through the monster's neck. Her head, jaw sputtering silent imprecations, landed crookedly at his feet.

Even before the rest of the body hit the ground, it was putrefying into black, hideous sludge. Despite himself, Losalis retreated a pace as the thing he'd just slain decayed into a thick morass that refused to mingle with the surrounding snows.

A tendril of fog flowed from the rotting form, skimming low over the white-shrouded earth, and then shot arrow-swift to the nearest corpse, the bloodless husk of one of Losalis's own men. He watched, pulse racing, as the mist slammed hard into the body, sending the corpse tumbling and rolling. Another instant, and it ceased thrashing, rolling smoothly to its feet, eyes open, mouth quirked in a malevolent grin. Haze hovered beneath its feet as it slowly, deliberately, advanced toward Losalis, a familiar spark of hell in its eyes. Losalis saw the skin tightening across its bones, growing pale as the remaining blood in the

*corpse was consumed by the thing that
rode it.*

*The Endless Legion. Finally, Losalis
understood.*

*With no shame in his heart, Losalis
called for a full retreat.*

(from *The Conqueror's Shadow*,
chapter twenty-one, Spectra, 2009)

Seeing those two passages together, it's pretty clear what kind of creature I'm describing, right? Drinks blood, turns to mist…Gotta be a vampire.

On the other hand, it doesn't have fangs; it's a body-thief; and its nature is a little less overt (at least at first) as presented over the course of the novel. If it's a vampire, it's not typical of the critters as they normally appear in fantasy or horror.

My point here—and it's one that most of you probably already know, but it's worth hitting anyway—is that including a standard genre trope doesn't mean that you have to approach it in the standard *way*. In Steven Brust's *Vlad Taltos* series, the main character is a human (Easterner) living among the Dragaerans. These are long-lived, tall, pointy-eared humanoids. Elves, right? But they're almost never called that (except as a racial slur by Easterners), and they don't act *anything* like the elves that Tolkien or *D&D* have made such a prevalent part of the genre. Moorcock's Elric was created, in part, as a deliberate inversion of the "mighty barbarian" trope most personified by Howard's Conan. The two characters are nothing alike, yet the archetype of one is directly responsible for the existence of the other.

Heck, the entire original Star Wars trilogy is arguably a fantasy, with its main tropes painted (sometimes quite lightly) in a veneer of science-fiction.

Depending on how thoroughly you disguise it, an altered trope can either be used to give the reader a sense of comfort or familiarity without quite knowing why, a nagging sense of something not being quite right, or just a moment of "Oh, cool! I see what you did there!" Of course, disguised *too* thoroughly, a trope might as well not be included at all. There's nothing wrong with changing a trope beyond recognition, using the familiar as a jumping-off point for the creation of something new; just be aware that that's what you're doing.

FALLING INTO CLICHÉ

A lot of you have been shaking your heads at me this whole time—don't think I can't see you, there in the back! And spit out that gum!—at my talk of tropes. You grumble and mutter something about clichéd, hackneyed writing.

And to an extent, you're right. It's easy, sometimes *very* easy, to slip from using tropes into clichés. Falling back on tropes, if done just because it's easier, leads to lazy writing. But that's not a good reason not to use them; just to be careful *how* and *why* you use them.

A trope becomes a cliché when it's used *in place of* other content, rather than as an *enhancement* of other content. Using the example of Corvis Rebaine as "fearsome armored warlord/black knight" from earlier, I used the classic imagery to introduce him, sure. But after that, the book delves into other aspects of the character: who he is, what he wants, why he does what he does. Had I relied *exclusively* (or even primarily) on the archetype— had "classic black knight" been the majority or the entirety of his character—then I would have slid down that slippery slope into the realm of cliché.

This is an *incredibly* easy mistake to make, especially when writing about traditionally heroic characters. The courtly knight—stalwart, brave, and true—is, frankly, a clichéd and uninteresting character. If, however, there's more to him, if there's something beneath the surface beyond more "stalwartiness," only then does he potentially become interesting. The mighty-thewed barbarian who makes his way by sword and axe is just a poor copy of Conan, *if* that's all there is to him. Motivations, personal foibles, quirks; these are what separate the characters from the clichés.

And again, this applies to the story as a whole, as well. If a tale involves a corrupt vizier who delivers the princess to the evil dragon, and the brave knight who must rescue her, *without* doing something unexpected or new with those tropes; if it involves the traditional human-elf-dwarf-halfling quartet of races without actually making some *use* of the racial differences or otherwise having a *purpose* for their inclusion; then yeah, tropes become clichés. But that's not the fault of the tropes themselves; it's the fault of poor writing, of using them as a crutch, or even as the entirety of a character or plot point, rather than a building block.

Some would say that certain tropes have been *so* overused that they are automatically clichés, and it can be tough to argue with them. I'm pretty lenient when it comes to such things, and even I roll my eyes when I come upon stories with the aforementioned orphaned farm boys growing up to be prophesied saviors. But I'd argue that even then, it's not *impossible* for an author to build something worthwhile on the trope—to do something new with it, or to use it as the starting point for an interestingly developed character—that keeps it from toppling over into cliché.

The character of Arlen in Peter V. Brett's *The Warded Man* is a good example. He's not a *precise* fit for this trope, but he's close enough that I initially sighed when coming across him in the book. Yet Brett very quickly took him and the story in directions that were different enough from the archetype that it ceased feeling clichéd almost instantly, and developed into a truly interesting character.

And "interesting," ultimately, is at the core of the entire point I'm making. Tropes in and of themselves? Not interesting enough to be relied upon; they are, in the end, nothing more than oft-repeated ideas. But as a *basis*

on which to build, as a means of communicating with—
and, yes, manipulating—the reader? There they come into
their own, there they make themselves useful. The best
fantasy writers aren't the ones who refuse to make use of
the tropes and archetypes of the genre; they're the ones
who know *when* to use them.

So You Want to Fight a War

PAUL KEARNEY

It's said that all effective drama revolves around conflict. Certainly this is true of personal relationships; who ever got excited reading about a happy couple that never argued? In fiction we want humanity to get a slap in the face, whether it's through crime, war, or good old kitchen-sink quarrels. It evokes in us both a feeling of empathy and a touch of schadenfreude. Sure, we want the guy to get the girl, the villain to get his comeuppance. But they must do a little dance for us first. They must get into each other's faces and mix it up a little for our entertainment. That's what keeps us turning the page.

Extrapolate that fact, and apply it to the fantasy genre. If an author has gone to the trouble of creating a whole invented world for his characters to bicker in and meander across, then the chances are that world will in some ways mirror our own, in diversity if nothing else. If a fantasy world does not have a serried assortment of races, creeds, philosophies and polities, then it's little more than an over-large ant farm.

Conflict, when it comes in such a milieu, may well blossom from interpersonal disagreement to the clash of arms. It may spiral up onto a grander stage. Whole nations and kingdoms may become involved. It's at that point the author must graduate from organizing a tap-room brawl to the consideration of armies, their raising, their deployment, and the ultimate depiction of them on the battlefield itself. How much detail the author puts into a burgeoning military campaign is entirely up to him or her and their personal approach to the depiction of mass violence. But no matter how blood-spattered the narrative becomes, in order for it to retain some kind of real-world integrity—in order for it to seem, for want of a better word, *realistic*—then there are certain factors that must be borne in mind.

> *A great rash spread over the desert, a river of men, dark under the sun save where the light caught the points of their spears. They raised a dustcloud behind and around them, a tawny, leaning giant, a toiling yellow storm bent on blotting out the western sky. It seemed a nation on the march, a whole people set on migrating to a better place. The sparse inhabitants of the Gadinai drew together, old feuds forgotten, and watched in wonder as the great column poured steadily onward, as unstoppable as the course of the sun. It was as grand as some harbinger of the world's end, a spectacle even the gods must see from their places amid the stars. So this, then, was the passage of an army.*
> (from *The Ten Thousand*,
> Solaris, 2008)

Armies. These are the ultimate instrument of state policy, and in the low-technology societies of most fantasy worlds, they are utilized to fulfill the ambitions of the state. This 'state' may well be driven by little more than the desires of one powerful man in a feudal setup, or it may reflect the wishes of some kind of popular assembly. It may merely be an aggregate bunch of mercenaries and ne'er-do-wells, or it may reflect some form of malevolent, nihilistic extra-worldly force, (a fantasy staple.) In any case, it is made up by a bunch of men or creatures that are armed and capable of mass maneuver, and usually there will be some form of hierarchy within it. An army cannot exist without officers of some form; without them, it is merely a mob, which is an entirely different thing.

Leaving aside the preternatural spawning of innumerable faceless hordes, an army of relatively 'normal' beings must be regarded in three different ways. Creation, subsistence, and deployment. Or to put it another way: how is it formed, how does it eat, and how does it fight?

You can sow dragon's teeth in the ground and have your battalions spring to instant life if you will, but most pre-modern armies had to be gathered together over a period of days, weeks, or even months. Men had to leave their homes and muster at prearranged locations, gathering incrementally, marching to ever larger concentrations, until finally the entire host was gathered together with its leadership and made ready to march as one giant entity. Think of the raising of the Rohirrim in *The Return of the King*. The bigger the army, the longer it will take to get it organized. And the larger the political entity that spawns it, the longer it will take men to come in from all the far flung corners of the land.

Even a professional, standing army, which were incredibly rare in pre-gunpowder history, will usually have to call in garrisons and outlying posts before it is formed up. Men will have to be equipped in some manner; either they will bring their own arms, or the state will supply them. Those who are light-armed cannot fight in the line beside the heavily armored; they will fall first and weaken the integrity of the formation. So there will be different types of units within the army, based on training and equipment. In both Rome and Greece, the poorer, less well equipped citizens fought as skirmishers, and the more prosperous farmers and tradesmen who could equip themselves with mail and shield and helmet formed the backbone of the phalanx or the legion. The richest of all owned horses, and these men formed the cavalry. Thus armies, even in notional democracies, were subdivided along lines of class and wealth.

Does your army have an elite? Of course it does—what self respecting fantasy author can resist the urge to emulate Leonidas and his Spartans, or Arthur and his knights?

The Persian Kings had a household guard of 10,000 men named the Immortals because their numbers were never allowed to fall below that level. The Thebans had the Sacred Band of 150 pairs of male lovers who fought and died like heroes under the hooves of Philip's cavalry at Chaeronea. Alexander had his Companions, Harold his Huscarles, the Byzantine emperors their Varangian Guard. In every ancient and medieval society the ruler has had a picked band of troops he relies upon for security, loyalty, and to stand fast when all around them are turning tail. Of such men are great stories made. Most armies have a cadre of hard cases like these, and an author would be missing an opportunity were he not to include them in his forces in some form. After all, some people have to be heroes.

Often, it is around these 'heroes' that the army accretes. Think of Joan of Arc, or William Wallace. While talking about massed armies and great campaigns, it's important, especially for our purposes, to remember that individuals made a real difference in pre-modern wars. Men cared about the leaders they served under, and would do extraordinary things for them. Alexander the Great is a glowing example of this. Yes, he was born Royal, but he made himself into a legend of his time through sheer brilliance. After him, men in emulation shaved their beards off for hundreds of years, and even tried to hold their head at the cocked angle which was typical of him. Mary Renault puts it beautifully, in the words of the aged Ptolemy:

He had a mystery. He could make anything
seem possible in which he himself believed.
And we did it too. His praise was precious,
for his trust we would have died; we did
impossible things. He was a man touched
by a god; we were only men who had been
touched by him; but we did not know it. We
too had performed miracles you see.
(from *Funeral Games*,
Pantheon Books, 1981)

In some ways, the hero counts for everything. He comes first, and can drag the rest of the fighting men behind him like the tail on a kite.

Let us say the hero and his army has been gathered together. Depending on the scale of the society involved the force can number in the hundreds or thousands. Imagine the numbers at a rock festival or a cup final, spread out across the countryside, all looking for somewhere to lay their heads. Those kinds of numbers can be sometimes hard to visualize, and the thought of trying to keep a grip of them all makes the head ache.

The camp of a good-sized army will not be small enough to look round at a glance; it will have the complexity of a city. Men will bed down beside those they know—neighbors or old comrades. Within the army there will be rivalries, even conflicts. Perhaps the host has gathered together contingents of men who were at one time at war with one another.

Now the nitty-gritty of the affair becomes ever more apparent. There's an old saying that amateurs discuss tactics, while professionals talk of logistics. The troubles of the army hierarchy have only just begun.

This horde of people must eat and excrete. Every day convoys of wheeled vehicles must be hauled into the camp, full of food, and in pre-modern times this food cannot be stockpiled as easily as in our refrigerated world;

there are no tin cans in most fantasy, and no portaloos either. Beef will be on the hoof, slaughtered in camp and then salted down or dried. Bread will have to be baked in situ. Staples such as corn, or lentils (which formed the mainstay of a Roman legionary's diet), will be consumed in stupefying quantities. Or perhaps the army will be more eastern in flavor, and will subsist on rice. In the Vietnam War the Vietcong lived on rice, a few vegetables, and dollops of fish sauce.

In any case, the need to feed the troops will to a large extent govern the maneuvering of the army. Will the host be able to live off the land of an enemy, or will it be campaigning in friendly territory? If it is to pillage as it advances then it will have to be weakened by sending out substantial foraging parties, and these detachments will in turn be vulnerable to ambush.

In camp another problem arises; sanitation. Ideally the army will encamp close to potable water, for the sake of the livestock as well as the troops. But think of the waste this great conglomeration of men and animals will produce. The camp will stink to high heaven. A disciplined, professional army will dig latrines, but most pre-technological armies simply squatted where they felt like it. In two or three days the army will be bivouacked in a cesspool, and if is summertime, disease will begin to nibble at the edges of the host's manpower.

This is something that is not covered by most fantasy writers, but I feel it to be key to the depiction of large-scale campaigning. After all, in almost every pre-modern war, more men died from disease than from enemy action. That was true right up to the end of the nineteenth century. It may be that the author does not wish to dwell on such prosaic details of military life; after all, we never see Aragorn popping out behind a bush before the uruks rush the Deeping Wall. It should at the back of his or her mind though. A large army encamped in one place for a long period will eventually succumb to sickness; that is reality.

(Unless they're elves, of course.)

So, the army has been gathered. It has been fed, and has a baggage train of wagons or pack animals which will keep the supplies coming forward. The men have dug latrines and are in rude health. Everything is tickety-boo. The author rubs his hands, thinking of the glorious Technicolor™ carnage to come, the fields of glory which await. The army is ready, finally, to march.

Have you ever been in a really, really long queue? Like you're trying to buy a Harry Potter ticket or an Apple gizmo on its first day of sale. When things finally get moving, the snake of people shuffles forward, and it can be an age before those at the back of the queue even register that the line is moving at all.

An army on the move is like that.

Think about how much space four men marching abreast will take up on a single-track road. They'll need six feet perhaps, so they don't tread on the heels of those in front. Now if you had ten thousand men marching four abreast, they would take up 15,000 feet, or a shade under three miles. Even if this mighty crocodile of men were to stand still, it would take an hour for a man to stroll from one end of it to the other.

Now imagine that the head of this column encounters the enemy. Even if it's a piffling little force of just a few hundred, those thousands back down the road will take many precious minutes to arrive on the scene, and in that time the men at the front of the long column will have been cut to pieces.

So the army cannot just march out in one big long line with our heroes resplendent at the head of it. It is at its most vulnerable in this formation, easily split up, and incredibly hard to concentrate against a threat. The sensible general will throw out flanking forces, preferably of faster moving light troops—perhaps even cavalry. He will have a forward guard of mounted men if he has them, and wide-ranging bodies of scouts scouring the land around. The army is a powerful instrument, but it cannot fight blind. Gathering intelligence on the surrounding region will enable the host's leaders to make better decisions when the time comes for the balloon to go up. And the outlying detachments will prevent the marching men from being taken by surprise.

Thus will the average soldier spend his day—trudging in a fog of sweat and dust with little to look at but the back of the man in front. Even if he is a horseman, he will be eating dust, (for nearly all campaigning must take place in the summer if the harvest or the spring planting are not to be interrupted.), and he will have a big horse steaming under him.

It has been estimated that even with all the advances in equipment and technology that our modern age has brought to warfare, the very minimum that a combat infantryman must carry on his back is some forty pounds. And that is moving light. Now think of what the crushing weight of an 80 pound mail shirt must have been like, or a bronze breastplate. And that's not taking into account a helmet, a sword or spear or both, a shield, and all the other myriad of equipment a man needs to make sleeping under the stars bearable. Men routinely carried upwards of 100 pounds on their back, and marched mile after mile under that load in all times of the year. In World War II, German infantrymen in Russia routinely marched forty miles a day. Stonewall Jackson's foot cavalry achieved something similar up and down the Shenandoah Valley. But by and large our army will be a lot slower. Depending on the size of it, and the cleverness of its commanders, it will be doing well to average half that. Xenophon thought that if an army made fifteen miles a day that was fairly adequate. Ancient armies were simply more unwieldy, and they were chained to a slow-moving baggage train of wagons that were more often than not pulled by plodding oxen. A column of cavalry might cut loose from its baggage for a time, and travel light, as Custer did on his way to the Bighorn, but it will suffer for it in broken down and played-out animals. And even Custer still had to take with him an ungainly and dilatory train of pack mules.

Finally this straggling behemoth makes its way to a place where it intends to meet its enemy. The location of the battle may be prearranged, either by tradition or geography. In classical Greece armies met and fought on the same fields for year on year, and even century upon century. Rocky, mountainous Greece had few level patches of open country that were deemed suitable for 'real' warfare, as opposed to the unsightly and unimportant skirmishing of lightly armed troops. So many battles were fought on the plains of Boeotia that it was called *the dancing floor of war*. Even closer to our own time, multiple battles were fought at such widely disparate places as Bull Run, and the Belgian Ardennes forest.

The ideal of pre-modern warfare is to meet the enemy in the field, and crush him decisively in one engagement. Anything else, and the war drags on, you have all those mouths to feed, and next year's harvest begins to look doubtful. Rome's professional standing army was unique in the Ancient world, in that it would fight year round, and would post its troops to any location regardless of their ethnicity. The men's loyalty was given to the legion and its commander, not to a tribal homeland, and, eventually, not even to Rome itself. (Therein lies the intrinsic danger of a standing army.)

Our author has brought his troops to the battlefield at last. Here we are at the tip of the spear, the consummation of all his scene-setting and plotting and conspiring. The grand spectacle of the battle itself awaits him. I find in writing battle scenes that to sit before an empty page on such occasions can be one of the most intimidating experiences in writing epic fantasy. This is the meat in the sandwich, and it has to be tasty.

One can talk about atmosphere, language, characterization and every other facet of the narrative.

This is still fiction; normal rules apply. But there are a few things that are different also.

> *Seated on his quiet mare, Vorus watched the line of spearmen march up the hill with a wall of sound that was the Paean preceding them. He thought he had never seen a sight so fearsome in his life: that moving battlement of scarlet and bronze, that wave of death approaching.*
> (from *The Ten Thousand,*
> Solaris, 2008)

Firstly, when the battle-lines clash, it's as well for an author to have an accurate idea of where exactly everyone stands. I always do what I do upon starting a fantasy novel—I draw a map. Write down the positions of the various forces, and the characters which are in those units. Note for sneering purists; it's not nerdy, and it doesn't reduce your magnum opus to the level of a *Dungeons & Dragons®* campaign.

Keep the map beside you as you write, and as the narrative progresses and the lines move and break and reform, annotate your map. By the end of the battle it should be covered in scrawls, but you will still see the sense within it. It should also have a scale, so that if you want one character to see another across that deadly space, you can gauge whether it's possible or not. Battlefields can be large places, miles wide. Our ten thousand men, standing in four ranks shoulder to shoulder, will form a line over a mile and a half long, and that's close-packed heavy infantry such as Greek spearmen or Roman legionaries. If your troops are wild-eyed Celtic types who like a lot of space to swing their swords, it will be even longer.

And you must know your troop types; what their purpose is and what they're capable of. If your much-caressed body of heavy cavalry go charging into the sunset in a haze of glory and horn-calls, and then meet a formed up body of disciplined spearmen, then you can kiss your magnificent cavalry charge goodbye. Horses—even trained destriers—will not gallop into a line of steady infantry.

However, if those spearmen flinch at the awe-inspiring sight of your hero and his mates bearing down on them, then there may be a chance. But by and large, cavalry want to be out on the flanks, feeling for the end of the enemy line. And your enemy, if he has any sense, will either meet your horsemen with his own, or anchor his flanks on unsuitable ground such as a wood or marsh where your hero's destrier will lose its momentum.

This is tactics, and it's not rocket science—in fact there is a kind of rock-paper-scissors sense to it. Spearmen counter cavalry but are vulnerable to missiles; they cannot get into contact with lightly armed skirmishers, who just scamper out of their way and thumb their noses at them. But skirmishers can be easily ridden down by cavalry.

If we delve deeper into the bloody contending lines of men on the battlefield, then we come to the very heart of the thing, what the Greeks called the *othismos*. Here is a massive scrum of flesh and metal and sharp pointy things.

> *The crash of the battle lines meeting, a sound to make the hearer flinch. It carried clear down the valley, and close on that unholy clash there came the following roar of close-quarter battle. The ten thousand Macht slammed into forty thousand Kefren like some force out of nature. In the rear of the Kefren left the archers loosed another volley, twenty thousand arrows overshooting to pepper the ground behind the Macht army. Before them, the ranks of their spearmen were shoved bodily backwards, pressing in on each other.*

Paul Kearney

147

Vorus could see the glittering aichme of the Macht darting forward and back at their bloody work all along the line, like teeth in some great machine, whilst the men in the rear ranks set their shields in the back of the man in front, dug their heels into the soft ground, and pushed. The Kefren phalanx staggered under that pressure, as a man's stomach will fold in on the strike of a fist. The battle line was simultaneously chopped to pieces and pushed in on itself. Vorus found the breath clicking in his throat. It had been a long time. He had forgotten what his people looked like in battle, and what savage efficiency they brought to war.

(from *The Ten Thousand*,
Solaris, 2008)

Lines will collide and come apart again. Crowds will coalesce and wither. Look at footage of riots on television. The riot police are the heavy troops, and the rioters are skirmishers. The riot police hold their line, but periodically charge forward when they've had enough things thrown at them. And to continue the analogy, the way mounted police make a crowd melt away in front of them as they charge must have something in common with the way pre-modern warriors once viewed bulky armored figures on big horses. The mere presence and bulk of all that meat and muscle counts for something, as much as the damage it deals out.

The Merduks in the valley looked up, and the Torunnans and Fimbrians who were fighting their desperate battle for survival saw a long line of cavalry come raging down from the hilltop like a scarlet avalanche. One thousand two hundred heavy horses carrying men in red iron, their lances a limbless forest against the sky, and that terrible, barbaric battle-hymn roaring down with them.

They sped into a gallop, their lines separating out, and the wicked lances came down from the vertical. The Merduk skirmishers took one look at that looming juggernaut, and began to run.

The first rank of the Cathedrallers rode them down, spearing them through their spines and galloping on. Half a dozen of the horsemen went down, their mounts tripping on the broken ground, but they closed the gaps and kept coming. The main Merduk formations below frantically tried to change their facings to meet this new, unlocked-for enemy clad in their own armor but glowing red as fresh blood and singing in some barbaric tongue. A regiment of Hraibadar arquebusiers stood to fire a volley, but the approaching maelstrom was too much for some of them to bear, and they ran also. Their formation was scrambled, even as the first rank of the Cathedrallers smashed into them.

The big horses rode down the Merduks as though they were a line of rabbits, and the terrible lances of the riders speared scores in the first clash. Horses went down, cartwheeling, screaming, crushing friend and foe alike, but the charge's momentum was too powerful to stop. They rode on, and behind them came the second rank, and the third, and the fourth. More horses falling, brought down by the corpses underfoot, their riders flung through the air to be trampled by the ranks behind them. Corfe lost sixty men in the

Paul Kearney

149

first thirty seconds, but the Merduks died
by the shrieking hundred.
(from *The Iron Wars*,
Ace, 2002)

The battlefield is a nasty place, and it would be rank dishonesty on the part of the author to suggest otherwise. I do not think that scenes of close combat should make for comfortable reading. I do believe that there can be moments of glory in warfare—too many soldiers have testified to the exhilaration of combat all through history for it not to be true. But I also believe that in the main, battle is an exhausting, horrific, terrifying experience, and no matter how many wands are waved or legions of flying monkeys descend, it should not be portrayed otherwise.

And your book will be the better for it.

Shit Happens in the Creation of Story, Including Unexpected Deaths, with Ample Digressions and Curious Asides

GLEN COOK

My first college roommate taught me several invaluable lessons about mundane life and demonstrated its profound connection to the Sea of Stories—though at the time he just pissed me off. His name was Gary. He hailed from Sarcoxie, Missouri, in the southwestern quarter of the state, geographically, historically, and culturally redneck Confederacy country. Gary was the first epileptic I ever knew, and the only professional bowler.

The boy was wicked good at rolling that ball. He had his own, too. Custom-drilled.

The first lesson he taught had to do with making character assumptions based on someone's background. Gary ran counter to stereotype, deeply. Though not particularly sophisticated he owned few of the prejudices, habits, or attitudes generally considered to be built into a country boy from his social pool. He was, in the main, indifferent to the social excitements of the Sixties. The one strong opinion I recall was an abiding disdain for the Beatles, their hairstyling in particular.

Gary favored a Marine Corps style cut. Too, he might have owned a certain level of jealousy based on the response of the female species to that posse of funny-talkers.

Dorms were tight in those days. We had another roommate, call him Jones. We three were packed into a space engineered for one back in the day of Spartan expectation that went with World War II. Jones was from Bowling Green, in northeastern Missouri: hard core Union territory. Jones demonstrated the character assumption rule, as well. He was as racist as they came. The moment he could do so he went Greek, to a house proudly flying the CSA battle standard instead of the US flag. He was no redneck. His people were local bankers, lawyers, and politicians, spanning generations.

(*Historical aside:* the **a)** Civil War, **b)** War for Southern Independence, was contested more bitterly in Missouri, though in battles of smaller scale, than most anywhere else, and defeat did not emotionally come home, for Confederacy sympathizers, until Jesse James was **a)** brought to justice, or, **b)** till that dirty little coward, Robert Ford, shot Mr. Howard, and laid poor Jesse in his grave.

On the other hand, our Confederates seem to have gotten over it more fully than have some in other locales.)

More importantly than showing me that the people within are not necessarily determined by what their outside circumstances would suggest, Gary taught me the relevance and importance of the connection of life to the title of this piece. I took it to heart, especially as regarded my own communion with the Sea of Stories.

Things happen outside causality. They do so in every life and, so, should in every plot. Unlikely shit happens every day, without warning, and has an impact on everything that comes afterward—often a lasting, history-determining impact.

On a hot August afternoon in 216 B. C. the protracted scheming and maneuvering of the Roman Senate brought the armies of Rome and its federates to contact with Hannibal at Cannae, in southern Italy. The plan was tactically and strategically sound. But...In three hours of intense fighting more people died than in any single day until the Tokyo firebombings of World War II more than two thousand years later. Rome suffered a defeat of a scale that we cannot even imagine today. Ten percent of the adult male, war-capable population of the Italian peninsula died that afternoon, yet still the battle, though it echoes and is still studied minutely today, was not decisive. Rome sucked it up and kept on fighting. The nearest to a 'Shit Happens' on that day was that a teenager named Scipio was one of the lucky survivors. Years later he would stand before the Senate after the Battle of Zama and declare, "Carthago delende est (*Carthage is no more*)!"

On June 10, 1190 the Holy Roman Emperor, Frederick I, called Barbarossa, leading as many as 100,000 to the Holy Land for the Third Crusade (a force that would have swamped the Muslim defenders), fell off his horse and drowned in the Saleph River before his men could pull him out. His army broke up. Only a few joined the kings of France and England for the fighting. Richard the Lionheart did a masterful job, smacking Saladin around real good, but the Third Crusade never had sufficient manpower to achieve its mission, which was the liberation of Jerusalem from the Saracen.

Shit happened 800 years ago. A man fell off a horse. The impact is still felt today.

Shit happens.

Early in our sophomore year, with no ominous behavior to give warning that shit was about to happen, Gary vanished. I mean, the man dropped off the face of the earth. After having borrowed every moochable cent possible off everyone he knew, during the course of one day, and after collecting as much cash as he could from the student loan office, he simply dematerialized. He stepped into the ether and even his family had no idea where he had gone, or why, or even if he were still alive. *Nobody* had a clue. There was no known girlfriend, no known trouble excluding maybe some questionable grades, nothing from which to run and nothing to which to run. Gary was there, then Gary was not there, and all that could be gotten out of it was that, shit happens.

Baffling, and soon enough forgotten, except in times when I really could have used the money I let him borrow.

Years later, after my time in the Navy, I was working assembly for General Motors and vigorously trying to make a personal connection with the Sea of Stories. One afternoon I decided to check the weather on a radio station I shunned normally as being nothing but boring talk for old farts. Shit happens. I caught a bit of the local news before the forecast. Well. One Gary Jay, of Sarcoxie, Missouri, had that morning been killed in a car crash on the Poplar Street Bridge complex that connects St. Louis to the Illinois side of the Mississippi River.

Insofar as I was ever able to determine this was the first time the man ever again came to the attention of anyone who knew him the day before he disappeared— though I will confess that I did not pursue the question with any passion. I never discovered where he had been or why he had gone there. I just knew, now, that I was no longer likely to get my money back.

I did internalize it all. I made it an important tool.

Shit happens.

Gary was a hole in the fabric of reality for seven years, then he stepped back in just long enough to let everyone know that he was going away for good.

At the time, and still, this strikes me as a gem straight off the floor of the Sea of Stories, the kind of thing not only useful in creating fiction but absolutely required. 'Random Shit Happens' is an uncomfortably fitting chunk of unpredictability belonging to a system my long-ago mentor Fritz Leiber called "ODThAA,' or 'One Damned

Thing After Another," approximating what science fiction author and editor Damon Knight termed, "Plotting by Intensive Re-complication." (A literary element of what, to quote contemporary philosopher Hannah Montana, can be described as, "Everybody has those days.") Though a bit more premeditated about it than I, Raymond Chandler demonstrated his affection for 'Shit Happens' by occasionally having a man with a gun bust through a door, thereby forcing himself to explain what that was all about and how it fit into his story.

(In Chandler's case 'Deliberate Shit Happens' was a device for getting a story going once it got caught on a seemingly unbreakable snag, prodding the Sea of Stories into giving something up.)

The Sea of Stories. I might ought to explain. In short, the Sea is the answer to that most annoying of questions, "Where do you get your ideas?" It is the universe outside the quotidian which yet encompasses both the mundane and the plane of the imagination. For me, at least metaphorically, all existence, and everything within it, is and always has been story. The Sea of Stories is where all the stories, and pieces of stories, are both born and are waiting to be found and written. There are lots and lots of stories. A finite number of storytellers at a finite number of computers (or other recording device, including the quill pen), will never drain the Sea of Stories dry, if only because the universe itself is finite in both space and time.

Bad things swim the Sea of Stories. So do good things, wondrous things, and nurturing things. And some of them manifest unexpectedly, with no warning. The Sea of Stories resembles life itself. Shit sometimes happens. More often than not, that is not good shit, because when good shit happens we do not really take notice. It is never part of a neatly polished, finely-tuned story arc. It is almost always an ambush, an IED alongside the literary road, planted by a cruel, maliciously insurgent fate. And then, like Raymond Chandler, you have to deal.

I find this absolutely essential for me in telling a story. I hope that it happens despite usually hating it when it aborts my great plans. I want my characters, on both sides of the divide (which will be exceeding vague at best), to be forced to cope with the unplanned and the unexpected. I want them to have to encounter, to face, to overcome, as they travel along the road to where they thought they wanted to go. Sometimes they will fail, as in life we do not always succeed when Fortune deals a surprise hand and changes everything forever.

I really hate it when shit happens to me in the real world.

I call myself an "intuitive" writer, meaning I connect with the Sea of Stories, then let the stories flow through and tell themselves. Not much planning goes into them. I don't do vast outlines or detailed character studies. I recognize a beginning, I dimly see a destination, and I start walking. The road to the end is a journey of discovery, nearly as full of surprises for me as I hope it will be for the reader coming to it blank. If it all goes completely right the characters will take over and do most of the story-channeling themselves. Still, elements of the story will present themselves by surprise. Referencing the title again.

The story itself determines everything, in the end. Even character, for true character can be demonstrated while dealing with the stress presented when we have to cope with the unexpected. (We Americans seem to be socialized to whine and demand that somebody else do something.)

The Sea of Stories is vast but finite. The simple act of selecting a piece of paper on which to begin commences a process of narrowing options and elements. Setting a first capital letter on paper instantly narrows all subsequent possibilities, and every word added confines the story even more. The occasional random stroke can make all the difference, adding sorrow, misery, certainly surprise, and, infrequently, a cherry on top of strawberry whipped cream.

In the latter context I am fond of referencing the appearance of the character known as the Dead Man early in the first book (*Sweet Silver Blues*, Roc, 1987) of my Garrett Files fantasy detective series, which originally strained to emerge from the Sea of Stories as a straightforward American P. I. novel. The Dead Man has appeared in every book since. He plays a major role in most, yet he was not planned and did not exist before something from the Sea compelled me to re-create *Sweet Silver* in a fantasy world. I was several chapters in, exploring the new vision. Detective Garrett had just endured a severe beat down. In its aftermath, entirely to my surprise, he announced that it was time to go see the Dead Man. When he arrived at that character's lurking place he found the Dead Man fully realized, complete with four hundred year back story, and prepared, lazily, to take his place as a lynchpin of the series.

Shit happens.

That time it was an out-of-nowhere burst from the Sea of Stories, a huge literary blast of the stuff.

Shit happens everywhere in my writing. It then shapes everything that comes after (and, often enough, redraws all that came before), on occasion to the point where everything else I write is shaped by having to account for one unforeseen event.

The most important, most critical place where 'Shit Happens' can impact a story is the unanticipated extinction of a critical character. Most writers are understandably loath to slay a favorite. I appreciate that completely, especially when that character is a favorite with readers. Readers can get quite upset when you do unseemly things to beloved imaginary friends. (And I love every second of that.) Some writers may strive mightily to evade the will of the Sea of Stories. They might contrive outrageously to satisfy the demands of readers unwilling to accept the truth. The classic example is the resurrection of Sherlock Holmes after events at the Reichenbach Falls.

I confess that some of my characters have returned, especially in the Black Company series. In those cases, though, honestly, they lied to me, too. Maybe the Sea itself was having fun tricking me, or just wanted me to believe so it would be easier to make the reader believe. I was convinced that they were gone, Soulcatcher being the premier and sneakiest old bitch to pull the stunt.

Few central characters perish in the Garrett series but not because that is set in stone. They can die. They will die if some bad shit happens.

Absolutely key and central characters die in the Dread Empire cycle, many assuredly not foreordained. When my fishing of the Sea of Stories fetches that shit up, though, there is nothing I can do to abort it. Trying to force things to go another direction, hammering and levering the story to conform to my emotional preference, only makes for a weaker or even outright bad story.

I cried, literally, while writing the passages where the character Mocker dies in *All Darkness Met* (Berkley, 1980). He was my favorite. I did not want him to go. I was desperate to find some means by which he could stay. But that just was not possible. Not while staying true to the story.

Mocker's passing in that book shaped every chapter in every Dread Empire book written since, be they set before or after his death. And, in a 'Shit Happens' event almost as potent and certainly as startlingly sudden as the manifestation of the Dead Man in *Sweet Silver Blues*, a series-shaping character perishes unexpectedly in *A Path to Coldness of Heart*, a new Dread Empire title eventually to appear from Night Shade Books. The relevant scene will be appended as an exemplar here. Consciously, for twenty-five years, I had much different plans for this man, a role as an abiding master villain.

There is a human nature aspect of 'Shit Happens' that needs addressing, that remains to be explored, which can be exploited to excellent effect, though I have not done a lot with it myself. That would be the fact that most people do not want to believe that shit happens. They are not emotionally equipped to accept randomness. The software in the wetware plain does not like 'Shit Happens,' particularly when the random smack from Fortune is a bad one. 'Shit Happens' is emotionally unfulfilling at the temporal site of the event.

The worse random shit is the more we want to make it have meaning, even if that is a secret Rosicrucian-*DaVinci Code*-Dealy Plaza sort of meaning. When shit happens we reject the declaration of insignificance so heartily that we invent vast, complex conspiracy theories in order to satisfy our need for meaning in what was really only irrational and random. A crazed lone gunman just does not provide emotional closure.

A rock just cannot plunge from the sky and kill your favorite sheep. Your family's survival may depend on that sheep making it through to the slaughtering season, or she may just be your special friend, but she cannot die for so slight a reason. There must be a malign entity or organization behind the arrival of that deadly stone: the Bavarian Illuminati, perhaps, or the Trilateral Commission, or Opus Dei, or God or the Girls Scouts. How about Skull and Bones? Jews? Communists? The Odessa. Fidel Castro. The US Air Force. You know who they are. Everybody out there is in on something, excepting you, and they are probably all against you.

There was a genuine, for real conspiracy involved in the Lincoln assassination, but it was not big enough and dastardly enough to suit the magnitude of the deed. Theorists have tried to ring in just about everybody from Jefferson Davis to Prince Albert since. A century and a half after the fact people still want to find a deeper, more eternal and cosmic meaning for what was, in reality, just another act of murder.

So, when the Sea of Stories delivers a Shit Happens sucker punch that shapes tomorrow and tomorrow forever it also hands over grand tools good for as much intensive re-complication as you care to indulge.

Your incident might not be as flashy or enduring as Roswell or Dealy Plaza, but a similar response is always triggered when shit happens and has a abiding emotional impact. Improbable theories always surface. A clever, crafty writer like you will find yourself able to get in there like a retrovirus and make it serve you.

Exploit whatever comes out of the Sea of Stories. Do not hold back. Slash and burn. When shit happens, exploit it down to the last whiff of the stink.

Your efforts will be just more leakage from the Sea of Stories anyway, perhaps slithering into minds unable or unwilling to recognize them for what they really are.

Unforeseen till just hours before they were recorded, the events chronicled in the following chapter opening changed everything that would happen in the Dread Empire world forevermore. It was convenient, too, in that it rendered this particular book (*A Path to Coldness of Heart*, Night Shade Books, 2012) much easier to complete in accordance with the publisher's wants.

Chapter Eight: Year 1017 A. F. E.: The Desert Kingdom

There was no wakening touch but Haroun knew one of his companions wanted his attention. A glance at the angle of the moonlight told him it was just after midnight. He heard harness creaks and horses' hooves. There was no need to whisper, "They're here."

Traveling by night.

Interesting.

Might be worth investigating.

Probably not worth the risk of exposure, though.

Haroun moved just enough to let it be known that he had heard.

He was *curious.*

He did nothing for several minutes. The sounds made by the travelers grew louder. They would reach the Sheyik's stronghold without coming near here.

Haroun had a premonition: It would not be wise to go look.

He rose, glided through the moonlight forty yards, slid into a shadow where his companions could not watch. He squatted, carefully extended his shaghûn senses.

The sounds of movement ceased.

Bin Yousif withdrew, cursing softly. Slight as his use of the power had been, it had been detected. A powerful someone accompanied the nightriders.

Up. Stride briskly back to his seat behind the tiny fire. Settle. Relax. Hope his companions did not ask uncomfortable questions.

Both were awake and nervous.

Shouting and order-giving began over yonder. Haroun concentrated on controlling his breathing.

A half dozen men trotted past. One paused to consider the derelicts. He wasted only a few seconds before moving on.

Haroun caressed the hilt of his favorite knife, gently, and wondered about the sorcerer who had detected his careful probe.

Another half dozen men rushed Haroun's former shadow from another direction.

Incomprehensible calls indicated that more men were coming.

Silhouettes glided into sight, following the half dozen who had passed by earlier, three in a loose wedge followed by a man who was nearly a giant.

Haroun did not think. He responded without calculation, lightning striking. He leapt onto the devil's back, left hand seizing his chin and pulling, right hand yanking his knife across the man's throat, slicing deep enough to cut the windpipe before the sorcerer could utter the first syllable of a protective spell. The slash cut all the way to the spine. Carotid and jugular spewed.

Bin Yousif threw himself clear, drove his knife into the belly of Magden Norath's nearest companion, who shrieked as he went down. He slashed another man's raised left arm. The third turned to run. He died from a thrust into his back.

Haroun ran the other direction after taking a moment to drive his knife into the sorcerer's left temple. He considered taking the head away, to destroy it a fragment at a time, but Norath's men had begun to react.

He became another shadow moving through shadows.

He was calm the whole time, from the moment he felt his knife slice Norath's esophagus. This was his life. This was what he had been born to do, till the day he made his lethal mistake. Cut, slash, stab, and walk away before anyone could respond.

Once out of sight he had serious advantages.

Norath's men could not know who they were hunting. He knew that anyone searching must be an enemy.

Magden Norath, though! How could that be? In his way, in his time, Norath had been as terrible as the Empire Destroyer. How could he have fallen so easily?

Norath had gotten sloppy. He had failed to protect himself because he had seen no need. Death had been on him before he knew he was in danger. It was the story of every mouse ever taken by an owl, fox, or snake.

Death was always one inattentive moment away.

Things began to prowl the night, hunting, things created by Magden Norath. Though hardly the savan dalage *the sorcerer had loosed during the Great Eastern Wars, they were formidable...*

The Reluctant Hero

ORSON SCOTT CARD

There is no human culture that does not value stories of heroes. Whether the heroes are gods, demigods, or mortals, ancestral or loose in time; whether they are conceived of as historical or fictional, we must have our heroes who exemplify the virtues we most admire.

Even in our supposedly post-heroic or anti-heroic literature, there is always an admirable hero. Anti-heroes are usually "anti" because they're anti-authority—in which case they're admirable as tricksters—or because they're of low birth, in which case they're Jack.

And in self-anointed "serious" literature (as if the rest of literature were playful, or about nothing), where the hero is definitely out of fashion, the hero has simply been displaced into the meta-story. The hero of *Lady Chatterly's Lover* is not *in* the novel; the hero is D.H. Lawrence, who heroically shattered the conventions of his time, making himself admirable to those looking for their heroes among the makers rather than the subject matter of literature.

Even if the author deliberately avoids anything that smacks of heroism or admirability, they're going to sneak into the story one way or another, because it is impossible to tell a story without, in effect, declaring what is important enough to be told about in story (or through the act of telling this particular story).

In other words, heroes cannot be avoided; they can only be disguised or displaced. Those who congratulate themselves on preferring post-heroic literature are merely deceiving themselves; indeed, they declare themselves to be heroes of a kind, because they do not need the heroes that common (or old, or dead, or ignorant) people need. However, not all heroes are created equal.

There are **heroes who seek to be heroic**—the great figures of epic who set out to lead Great Lives, like Achilles, a petulant god-chosen child of warfare. Brave in battle? Highly skilled at killing? Yes and yes. Glory-seeking, pouty, and utterly selfish? Yes again, and again, and again. By our moral code, at least.

Achilles is a hero of a Heroic Age, who is conceived of by people living in a definitely non-heroic age (us) as being not only aware of his undying fame, but desirous of it. In our era, we regard fame-seeking as somewhat needy—and yet people openly do outrageous, demeaning things merely to be seen by many.

Inhabitants of Heroic Ages—and the storytellers and audiences who celebrate them—include among the heroic virtues that of desiring Good Fame. When you think of it, this is actually one of the fundamental virtues of civilization. Selfish and brutal as Knights in Shining Armor or demigods might be, the very fact that they care so very much about what their community thinks of them—their reputation—reminds the audience that even the great seek something that only the community can give them, and will sacrifice much to obtain it.

Policemen and firemen, soldiers and military seamen and pilots are the far-more-altruistic successors of heroes who seek to be heroes. They don't seek their own death, but they choose to risk it in order to save or protect others, and honor is their highest reward, in part because they volunteered, and in part because their heroism is in the service of the community. They are Heroes by Career.

But in all times and places, communities also value—and often value more—the hero who does not choose himself.

It can be the **hero of circumstance**: The unidentified man from Air Florida Flight 90 when it crashed into the icy Potomac River on 13 January 1982, who stayed in the water helping other survivors get to the lifelines dropped by helicopters, until all were saved but him—he did not board that flight intending to be a hero. Chance put him in the way of heroism, and he acted upon the noble impulse.

Or the mostly unidentified heroes of Flight 93, who, once they learned that their hijackers intended to crash the plane where it would kill many other people, attempted to take back the plane; they died, but saved many lives.

How did any of these heroes know that such nobility was expected of them? *Because they had absorbed so many hero stories in the past.* They were acting out the script that they had learned over and over, which told them that "greater love hath no man than this, that he lay down his life for his friends"—or, in more quotidian terms, the survival of the community depends on the sacrifices of citizens when called upon.

The heroic acts of the heroes of circumstance are chosen in the moment when action must be taken, or not. Either you snatch the stranger from the burning car now, or it will be too late. Act or don't act—it is all over in a few moments.

But the great fantasy literature of today is largely built around heroes who never wanted to be heroic, and who have plenty of time to equivocate, to change their minds, to pass along the burden to others, or to misuse their heroic role.

The **reluctant hero** says, "O my Father, if it be possible, let this cup pass from me: nevertheless not as I will, but as thou wilt." Or, in other words, "I will take the Ring to Mordor, though I do not know the way."

Is this a mere formula? In the hands of uninspired or untalented writers, of course it is. How many very-bad movies have we seen where the hero keeps coyly saying no until he finally says yes, or until he's forced into it?

But the formulaic reluctant hero is a bit of a fraud, and we are not satisfied. Why? Because if he is truly forced into his heroic action, it isn't heroism at all, is it? Or if he is given a deeply personal incentive, his heroism becomes self-interest.

I think of the horrible moment in the botched movie *The Rock*, in which Nicolas Cage has to save San Francisco from a biological death agent. That was his job—he is in the fireman category of hero. But the hackmeisters of Hollywood (either the writers or the executives who defile their work) decided that saving a million people just wasn't enough jeopardy. So the script has Nicolas Cage's lover happen to arrive in the danger zone, so now if he fails, she dies.

The audience groaned aloud, not out of empathy but in disgust. The filmmakers, utterly ignorant as they were of how storytelling actually worked, had increased the jeopardy, but at the cost of virtually negating Cage's heroism. Now instead of risking death to save the community—heroism—he was risking death to save his main squeeze, his primary reproductive opportunity. Now his urgency isn't noble, it's practical.

We might call people who save their spouses or children heroes, but we don't emotionally group them with the heroes who gave or risked their lives for *strangers*. They are brave, but their motivation is personal, not public. If they failed to act, they would be among the primary sufferers; they are sparing themselves.

The essence of the true reluctant hero is that he is *not acting primarily to save himself* or those closest to him. He is acting to save a larger community—even the entire human race or the whole world—from a dire threat. He is reluctant to do the heroic deed in part because it is *not* personal. His own stake in the matter is no more than that of most other people in his community, and yet he must step into a situation that usually offers no plausible escape once he has done the noble deed.

If he does not want to be a hero, and has no personal stake, and he did not choose a risky heroic profession, how *does* a reluctant hero get tapped for the job? He feels entitled to say, Why me? Why not someone who has trained and prepared for it?

Gandalf has no better answer for Frodo than that he thinks somehow Frodo was "meant" to carry the Ring. (Catholic Tolkien was being coy; he didn't call the one who chose Frodo "God" but that is clearly what was intended, as *The Silmarillion* makes clear.) It is the prophet Jeremiah: "Before I formed thee in the belly I knew thee; and before thou camest forth out of the womb I sanctified thee, and I ordained thee a prophet unto the nations."

When God or the gods choose you, Oedipus, there's no escaping it; not even your parents can spare you from it.

In other stories, it's an accident of birth (as it partly is in Frodo's case, being the favorite nephew of the childless Bilbo, and thus the heir to Bilbo's found-yet-also-stolen Ring). Hereditary kings often make the claim, "I never chose this, I didn't ask to be king."

Indeed, 2010's Oscar winner for best picture, *The King's Speech*, makes a reluctant hero of King George VI by stressing again and again how little he wants to be king, yet how desperately his country needs him to inspire them by speaking well. (In fact, England had someone who did a far better job of inspiring them—Winston Churchill—so that the king could have been a Popsicle stick for all his speaking ability mattered.) Also, the film made everybody aware of the inevitability of World War II at a time when Winston Churchill was almost the only person of prominence taking the possibility seriously.

In short, the fictionalization of the otherwise accurate *The King's Speech* was devoted mostly to making it clear why George VI's labors to overcome his stammer were not for personal ends—*he* was happy to be a private man—but rather altruistic, for the good of the nation, required of him because he happened to be the younger

Orson Scott Card

169

brother of a man too idiotic to be King of England (a bar which was already set very low indeed).

Whether it's God, gods, fate, or birth, it is important that the reluctant hero has his heroic opportunity thrust upon him. And yet he must *choose to embrace it.* The reluctant hero does not wish for heroism, but when he sees the need, and the fact that no one else is likely or willing to do what must be done for the sake of all, he grasps the nettle firmly and holds on till the end.

I had no idea of this whole hero business when I started my writing career. I was vaguely aware of Joseph Campbell—but only in the way I was aware of Ayn Rand, as the author of occasionally interesting nonsense. I had no intention of writing mythic heroes. I meant only to write stories that I believed in and cared about, with endings that satisfied me.

And I submit that this is the way the great stories come about. When writers attempt to create heroes using formulas, there is an indelible stamp of insincerity that cannot be wiped away. The heroic balance between reluctance and willingness is such a delicate one that the insincere writer, throwing formulas on one side or another of the scale, is bound to get it wrong.

Only the true believer in the heroic myth, unconscious of how that belief is controlling his story choices, can find his way to a satisfactory—and, on rare occasions, a perfect—balance.

In the tradition of the reluctant hero, in writing this essay I was loath to use my own stories as examples. Partly that reluctance is due to my experience with authors who can talk about nothing but their own stories. Back when I used to go to science fiction and fantasy conventions, I made it my private code to avoid referring to my own work, taking all my good examples from the work of others.

(This was not heroic sacrifice; my policy spared me the embarrassment of realizing that nobody in the audience was at all familiar with my work, and I avoided annoying audience members with authorial self-obsession, thereby making them more likely to buy my books. Self-interest was the handmaiden of modesty.)

But the editor reminded me that the point of this book is for the practitioners of Heroic Fantasy to talk about what they themselves have done. Even so, I really meant it when I said that I was completely unconscious of my own process of hero creation. I did not examine it for fear that I would kill it by laying it out on the examining table. How could I write about something that I had studiously avoided studying—the creation of the hero in my own work?

Fortunately, I came to write this essay precisely at the time that I was struggling to write yet another draft of the screenplay of my own novels *Ender's Game* and *Ender's Shadow*. Time and again, I and other writers had proven that whatever made Ender Wiggin an indelible hero to many readers was devilishly hard to bring to life in another medium.

We blamed the difficulty on translating the deep penetration of novelistic viewpoint to the absolutely shallow penetration of the screen. And that has certainly been a challenge. But ultimately, the problem was that nobody understood why Ender Wiggin was an effective, memorable hero—least of all me.

Ender's Game is not fantasy; it is not a useful prop for this essay. But the things I learned, at long last, in writing this draft of that screenplay apply across the board. I can find the same elements now in all my effective heroes (we will, mercifully, leave the ineffective ones in the corner and largely ignore them, like incontinent or flatulent relatives).

Let's take Alvin Miller, of *The Tales of Alvin Maker*. I started with his birth, and if the first five chapters establish anything, it's that Alvin, as the seventh son of a seventh son, has greatness thrust upon him. Chosen from conception, his fate is watched over by a little girl who eventually grows up to become his wife. She sees the many possible fates that lie before him—as long as she continues to act to keep him alive.

Yet as Alvin grows up and discovers his intense magical powers, he still has choices, and at a key moment he takes responsibility for the consequences of his magical deeds. Like many a child, he is a prankster and his siblings become the deserving targets of his pranks. Alvin uses his power to persuade cockroaches to swarm all over his offending sisters—but as they stomp the roaches to death, Alvin feels those tiny deaths and realizes that he has led them to slaughter solely for his own amusement, for the pleasure of petty vengeance for a petty offense.

He takes a vow never to use his power for his own benefit again. From now on, he will act only to help others—his family, his friends, his community, utter strangers—but never himself.

Naturally, the story bends around to a decision point where that vow, if he keeps it, will lead directly to his own death, because he has an infection which will kill him, and which only he has the power to heal. This is how I morally torment my characters: Whatever they have righteously decided is the right thing to do, I make impossible; whatever they regard as utterly wrong, I require it of them.

I never consciously set out to be that writer; it's just what felt right to me. It was never a "theme"—I despise deliberately chosen themes as part of storytelling; they belong in essays and should stay there. Apparently, however, there is something in my own unconscious conception of how the universe works that makes it so moral rectitude is never responsive to clear, clean lines. As soon as my hero draws a circle and stands within it, I set the circle on fire and force him to find a way back out of it, without destroying himself in the process.

Because somehow—again without forethought on my part—I find a way for the reluctant hero to remain heroic.

And, sad to say, it almost always amounts to this: Others will go into the Promised Land, Moses, but never you. Ender Wiggin saves the human race, but cannot ever return to Earth. Alvin Miller saves his own life, but only at the cost of an unbreakable vow that his life was only worth saving if he devotes it entirely to defeating the Unmaker, who cannot be defeated. His wife, who sees the future, understands that the path he has chosen leads almost inevitably to his own death and to the failure of all his enterprises—and yet she also sees that this is the only path that he can follow and still be the kind of man he aspires to be.

The Tales of Alvin Maker is an epic, and I have not yet finished it; but, as I have been telling people for years, my ultimate source material requires that the series will end with Alvin murdered, his body lying on the streets of Carthage City, while other, lesser makers try to carry on his work. It is the only way, source material or not, that the story *can* end. Because it is the only way that Alvin can choose to fulfill the heroic role that was thrust upon him, without defiling the purity of his heroism.

Purity—I have met a few people in my life who are truly pure in heart, or so I believe; but I am not one of them. Alvin is not "pure"; I write no Galahads. I say only that his *heroism* is pure, because he loses all that he has for the sake of the larger community, and carries nothing away but his virtue, and leaves nothing behind but his love and teaching.

So let me turn to a hero of mine who is not so pure: Ivan Smetski, from the novel *Enchantment*. He grew up in Ukraine under the old USSR; by "chance," as a child, he was running through the woods and saw a beautiful woman asleep within a sea of leaves: It was Sleeping Beauty. There was also a monster in the leaves around her, and he fled.

His family emigrated to the United States and he became an American—but he never forgets the woman in the leaves, and when the USSR falls, he goes back to Ukraine as a grad student researching folklore. He returns

Orson Scott Card

173

to the site and finds the woman, still guarded by a magical bear; he bravely gets to her, kisses her, wakens her, goes back with her to her kingdom in the distant past of Russia…

And then discovers he is in a Russian folktale, which means that the young man marries the princess, yes, but he does *not* live happily ever after, because she doesn't like having been given in marriage to a commoner, and tries to kill him.

They work it out, after he gets her to the America of today for a while, and they eventually fall in love, save her ancient kingdom from Baba Yaga, and all kinds of magical things. (I am overly proud, I fear, of having turned Baba Yaga's hut-on-legs into a hijacked 747.)

So what kind of hero is Ivan Smetski? He finds out in the course of the story that nothing he did was really by chance—he was manipulated again and again without realizing it at the time. Yet he also made the heroic choice, and more than once.

One of the elements of the true Reluctant Hero is that his heroic choice is made in full awareness, not of all possible consequences, but of the strong likelihood that things will End Badly for him. Ivan's first choice, to waken the sleeping woman, is the act of a Hero of Circumstance: There she is, he thinks she's endangered by the bear, and certainly she's under a magical spell which he has the power to lift. He acts at once because it's either that or act not at all. Only afterward does he find that he has unwittingly set himself on a path fraught with dangers magical, political, and personal.

Later, when he falls in love with this stranger that he wakened and married on impulse (when you're caught in a fairytale, don't you just go with it?), he is tossed to and fro by circumstance. Eventually they fall in love and make the marriage real. But he is not so much a hero as a man desperately trying to escape the consequences of his previous choices.

It is only near the end of the book that he once again faces a heroic choice—but it is not really his. All of

Princess Katerina's actions, including her marriage to Ivan, have been prompted by her responsibility as daughter of the king of ancient Taina. Marrying him was *her* sacrifice for the sake of the kingdom, to keep it from being taken over by the utter evil of Baba Yaga.

Katerina had already made her choice, and never wavers. When Ivan falls in love with his wife and seeks to make their marriage real, he knows that he is not marrying a woman, he is marrying a kingdom as personified by the woman. He will have to take responsibility, along with her, for saving the kingdom.

So is his heroic choice—reluctant though he has certainly been—pure in its heroism? He takes upon himself the burden of the kingdom, but he also gets the love of the woman he loves. So when he risks death by facing Baba Yaga in her lair, is he doing it to save the kingdom, or to please his lady?

One might say that it makes no difference—but in creating a literary hero, the difference is huge. But remember, I like to blur all those crisp, clean lines. He has come to accept personal responsibility for the kingdom; he does not act for Katerina's sake alone. Yet he *does* act partly for her sake as well. He is not pure.

Which is just as well, because in the end it was not that particular heroic choice that saves him. In fact, he comes to understand that while his role in it was vital, even central, he is not really the hero of his own story. Someone else is. And yet, because he never wanted to be a hero, he is content to find out that he was someone else's tool for much of his life. The outcome of all is a good one, and he was brave and self-sacrificing when such deeds were called for. But he didn't have to die.

He still pays a price. His children, when they are born, must choose between the America of today and the Taina of their mother's past; eventually the bridge between the times and places will close, and those who are trapped on one side without being able to see those on the other will grieve. The loss is real. Yet the children themselves, though they might be lost at some future date, are also

Ivan's and Katerina's reward. Yes, the kingdom was saved; yes, they are rulers there, and good ones, as best they can manage it. But their love, and the children born of it, are the "happily ever after" that they get despite the fact that this is a Russian story; it is also half American, and we must have our happy endings.

So…is Ivan Smetski a Reluctant Hero? He certainly does not pick himself for a heroic life, but his first heroic choice is that of a Hero of Circumstance, and his second one is "tainted" by the fact that he is motivated at least in part—and probably in largest part—by his love for Katerina.

She also is a hero chosen by fate—she was born royal—but she fully embraced her heroic role and willingly embarked on whatever that role required of her. She is a hero, but not a reluctant one: she is a Hero by Career.

Ultimately, then, *Enchantment* is more love story than hero story. There are heroes in it, and Ivan's reluctance is attested on many pages. But in the end, it did not all rest entirely on his shoulders, as it did with Ender Wiggin and will, when I finish his story, with Alvin Maker.

So let me give you perhaps the purest Reluctant Hero to be contained within the pages of a single volume of my writing: Mack Street, the hero of *Magic Street*.

I began that novel on a kind of dare. A friend of mine, Roland Bernard Brown, wrote to me at the very beginning of our friendship that he wanted me to write a hero who was an American Black male. I was certainly a reluctant writer—I knew well the pitfalls that await a writer who tries to write a story inside a culture he does not belong to. But Roland helped me greatly, and there's also the fact that humans are humans; I think *Magic Street* may well be my best novel.

Set in the upper-middle-class black Los Angeles neighborhood of Baldwin Hills, the story of Mack Street shows him as a magical child, conceived under circumstances reminiscent of the Virgin Birth…and *Rosemary's Baby*. He grows up innocent as a wandering child; he has a home, but he is also adopted by the entire neighborhood, becoming a child of community.

Gradually, though, he realizes that the magic that is erupting into the world through a place in Baldwin Hills is uniquely his problem to contain and control. People are dying or losing all they love, and only Mack can stop it. Truly his role was thrust upon him, by birth and by his unique ability to solve a problem; but he is also deeply reluctant. He never sought heroism. He was *happy* and his life was good, and solving the problem will end all hope of happiness for him, though he does not understand, when he makes his choice, quite why.

When it becomes clear that his very life is part of the cause of the dire evil that has befallen the community he loves, there is only one solution: To end that life. And he embraces the choice, extinguishing himself and his hope of happiness. That he doesn't actually die, that there is a person who remembers having been Mack Street, is beside the point. The life of Mack Street is over, and it was a good life, but to continue it would have meant that others would pay a high price in misery and loss. For Mack, that would not have been happiness. So no matter what he chose, his happiness was over; he chose, then, to give up his freedom, his self, for the sake of all.

For many years my wife and I kept the slogan "Noble Romantic Tragedy" on little signs stuck to walls in various rooms of the house, so that I could keep focused on what I aspired to write. With *Enchantment* I came very close; with *Magic Street* I think I achieved it. And now, writing this essay, I suspect that much of what puts *Magic Street* across that fine but all-important line is the fact that Mack Street is my most perfect Reluctant Hero.

So now that I've said all this, what have I accomplished? Is this a formula that you can follow? Oh, I hope not. I hope you will learn the other lesson, that it is what you unconsciously care about and believe in that will make your stories most powerful and truthful. And yet it will

Orson Scott Card

177

not hurt a thing if you are aware of these elements of the Reluctant Hero, as long as you never distort your fiction to achieve them. Tell the story that feels true and important to you, regardless of rules or formulas or mythic patterns or archetypes; they only work when they are unconsciously followed.

My worry is that every time I articulate a rule, I then set out to break it. When I told students at Elon College to avoid suicide stories, and stories in first person present tense, what did I do but go home and write a tale told in first person present tense by a man who has just blown his own head off with a shotgun? I'm afraid I can't escape my own determination to flout authority, even when the authority I'm flouting is my own.

Yet I also know I have no need to worry, because as I have also said here, it is impossible to write stories without a hero, even when you try. You will subvert your own effort without even knowing that you were doing it until after—if you ever realize it at all. And what's true of you will be true of me. I have warned you that you will fail if you try to follow these observations like a formula; but I warn myself along with you that we will also fail if we try to violate the formula by creating its opposite. Unless you truly do not care about your work, you cannot make it heroless; and, to be frank, I believe that even those who swear they do not care, that their art is just a game that means nothing to them are fooling themselves. You cannot tell a story without coming to care for it, even if you meant not to; and to the degree you care about it, you will use it to tell some truth, even if you think you don't believe that anything is true. It's built into us hairless big-headed primates, a primitive need that expresses itself, for some reason, in hero stories, which we cannot live without and still be human.

Afterword

The mythologies and pantheons of every culture and belief system were filled with super men before there was *a* Superman. We humans have always been fascinated by heroes. We require them to give us hope—and targets at which to aim. We expect them to be heroic—yet are a little bit surprised every time they are; we demand they triumph—yet are slightly disappointed when they do. We're grateful—and jealous. This is what makes heroes addictive, for we oblige them to be us and simultaneously more than we can (believe ourselves to) be. En masse and individually.

We thrive on tales of heroics. Across every culture, through every era, we speak of heroes. Ever since that first person stepped into the gap, prepared to risk it all on behalf of something more and saved the moment, we've been talking about them. Looking to them. Praising them. Creating them. Being them. Yet most of all: sharing them.

Doing so uplifts us and binds us as a people, for we innately need each other to share these stories of admirable individuals with motivations and deeds that all of us can aspire to.

Share them we have, through every medium of communication: oral traditions to movies, biographies to campfire tales, hieroglyphics to video games, song and verse and art to finger puppets, sand sculptures and tattoos. Heroes are in our myths, legends, folklores, morals, creeds and fairy tales. They are created and learned of by adults and children...and believed in, trusted, and imitated by all.

The sharing of heroes infuses the marrow of our life.

Yet the *telling* of them is but the universal third of it; there is also the *being* and the *creating*. This being, of course, is what it's all about, for without the actual deeds of heroes—why, we would have none. Ah, but it's the final third of which we've just read, that bit about the creating of our heroes that churns within the souls of many…of you. Do the words embodying all that *you* hold heroic burn within, seek release through your fingertips and lips?

Writing Fantasy Heroes gathers the expertise of recognized storytellers; professionals with well-known and adored heroes come to share from their wells of knowledge and experience, and provide the tools and attitudes crucial to sharing those heroes. They cannot create for you though. Only you can bring your heroes. You write their deeds; you deliver their tales to the world. It's your turn to create our heroes.

So what does make a hero?

He or she is the embodiment of mankind's desire to save itself. The iconic figure of our hopes to be more in the face of the worst that can be done to us…even by us. Often in spite of our personal desires and despite our inclinations. Aragorn succeeds as hero not because he sought to—but in direct opposition to his own hopes and desires…and fears. Conan is heroic not because he wishes to be—but directly as a result of his ill-favored desires, his pursuit of wealth, women, and wine…and his contempt for the barbarity of 'civilized' man. Heroes—reluctant or not, intentional or not—save the regular people and succeed in doing 'good.'

'Good' matters. And we want someone to *do good* by each of us. Thus, saving us regular people is good and heroic. As is giving us values, such as what it means to trust and be trusted, to be brave; what courage looks like, and that honor and truth can resonate deep within us. Heroism sings to us of what it means to be human and its song is powerful.

Why a book about *Fantasy Heroes* though? Epic battles, awesome weapons, untamed magics, fearsome warriors—fantasy is more than all of these. It is a reflection of our world and time minus the cloudiness of contemporary realities and preconceptions—and it fires the imagination to expand and embrace concepts lacking or unbelievable in our current life. Escapism? Not a chance. I despise that description: I name it *Freedom*.

David Gemmell would have been a splendid inclusion to this book. A master of heroic fantasy, his untimely death in 2006 robbed us of the opportunity. After his death, James Barclay commented:

> *David believed in the great strengths of humans and their capacity to defeat evil and save good. He reflected those strengths in his novels as well as in everything that he said...while [he believed] it was almost impossible to define 'heroism' so far as he was concerned, there was one thing he always bore in mind. And it was this: that when for all others, all hope is gone and despair and defeat are inevitable, for a hero, there is always something that can be done.*

Keep sharing your heroes—for we're only as good as they are.

Jason

Jason M Waltz
Milwaukee, WI, USA
December, 2012

Afterword

181

Contributors

Biographies, photographs, and selected bibliographies,
were provided by the contributors:

ALEX BLEDSOE

JENNIFER BROZEK

ORSON SCOTT CARD

GLEN COOK

DLEOBLACK

STEVEN ERIKSON

IAN C. ESSLEMONT

CECELIA HOLLAND

HOWARD ANDREW JONES

PAUL KEARNEY

ARI MARMELL

JANET AND CHRIS MORRIS

CAT RAMBO

BRANDON SANDERSON

JASON M WALTZ

C. L. WERNER

Alex Bledsoe

Eddie LaCrosse novels:
The Sword-Edged Blonde (2007)
Burn Me Deadly (2009)
Dark Jenny (2011)
Wake of the Bloody Angel (2012)

Tufa novels:
The Hum and the Shiver (2011)
Wisp of a Thing (2013)

Memphis Vampsloitation novels:
Blood Groove (2008)
The Girls with Games of Blood
(2010)

Firefly Witch chapbooks:
The Firefly Witch (2012)
Croaked (2012)
Back Atcha (2012)

Collection:
Time of the Season: Three
Holiday Stories (2012)

Alex Bledsoe grew up in West Tennessee an hour north of Graceland (home of Elvis) and twenty minutes from Nutbush (birthplace of Tina Turner). He now lives in a Wisconsin town famous for trolls. Find more about Alex at www.alexbledsoe.com.

Jennifer Brozek

Selected collections:
In a Gilded Light (2010)
Karen Wilson Chronicles (2012)

Selected novels:
The Lady of Seeking in the City
of Waiting (2012)

Selected nonfiction:
Industry Talk (2012)

Jennifer Brozek is an award winning editor, game designer, and author. Winner of the Australian Shadows Award for best edited publication, Jennifer has edited ten anthologies with more on the way. She has more than fifty published short stories, and is the Creative Director of Apocalypse Ink Productions. Jennifer also is a freelance author for numerous RPG companies. Winner of both the Origins and the ENnie award, her contributions to RPG sourcebooks include *Dragonlance, Colonial Gothic, Shadowrun, Serenity, Savage Worlds*, and White Wolf SAS. Jennifer is also the author of the long running *Battletech* webseries, *The Nellus Academy Incident*. When she is not writing her heart out, she is gallivanting around the Pacific Northwest in its wonderfully mercurial weather. Jennifer is an active member of SFWA, HWA, and IAMTW. Read more about her at www.jenniferbrozek.com.

Orson Scott Card

Ender's Game series (begins with):
Ender's Game (1985)
Speaker for the Dead (1986)

The Tales of Alvin Maker (begins with):
Seventh Son (1987)
Red Prophet (1988)

The Women of Genesis (begins with):
Sarah (2000)
Rebekah (2001)

Pathfinder novels:
Pathfinder (2010)
Ruins (2012)

Selected novels:
Enchantment (1999)
Magic Street (2005)

Selected nonfiction:
Characters & Viewpoint (1988)
How to Write Science Fiction and Fantasy (1990)

Orson Scott Card was born in Washington and grew up in California, Arizona, and Utah. He served a mission for the LDS Church in Brazil in the early 1970s. Besides his writing, he teaches occasional classes and workshops and directs plays. He recently began a long-term position as a professor of writing and literature at Southern Virginia University. Orson currently lives in Greensboro, North Carolina, with his wife, Kristine Allen Card, and their youngest child, Zina Margaret. Find out more about Orson Scott Card at www.hatrack.com.

Glen Cook

The Garrett Files (begins with):
Sweet Silver Blues (1987)
Bitter Gold Hearts (1988)

The Black Company (begins with):
The Black Company (1984)
Shadows Linger (1984)
The White Rose (1985)

The Dread Empire (begins with):
A Shadow of All Night Falling (1979)
October's Baby (1980)
All Darkness Met (1980)

Instrumentalities of the Night novels:
The Tyranny of the Night (2005)
Lord of the Silent Kingdom (2007)
Surrender to the Will of the Night (2010)

Selected novels:
The Swordbearer (1982)
Sung in Blood (1992)

Glen Cook was born in New York City, lived in Indiana briefly, grew up in Northern California. He attended the University of Missouri, served in the U.S. Navy, then worked for General Motors in various capacities until he retired to become a fulltime writer. Author of nearly 50 books, he is best known for his *Black Company* and *Garrett Files* novels. He lives in St. Louis, Missouri. Glenn is pictured above with his grandson Joshua.

Dleoblack

Dleoblack is a freelance illustrator, working in digital medium, and skilled in fantasy art. Visit his online portfolio at www.dleoblack.deviantart.com and contact him at www.dleoblack.com.

Steven Erikson

Learn about Steven and the world of *The Malazan Book of the Fallen* he co-writes in with Ian C. Esslemont at www.stevenerikson.com and www.malazanempire.com.

Ian C. Esslemont

Novels of the Malazan Empire:
Night of Knives (2004)
Return of the Crimson Guard (2008)
Stonewielder (2010)
Orb Sceptre Throne (2012)
Blood and Bone (2013)

Ian C. Esslemont grew up in Winnipeg, Canada, where the flat prairie heartland meets the boreal forest. His first degree was in archaeology and he worked on sites in Ontario and Manitoba. It was on these crews that he met fellow writing and fantasy genre enthusiast Steven Erikson. The two then drove cross-country to Victoria, British Columbia, where they attended a creative writing program, roomed together, and wrote, talked and gamed in the fantasy genre far more than they really ought to have.

After graduating from Victoria, Ian drove four thousand kilometers from Winnipeg to Fairbanks, Alaska, in a Dodge Colt two-door manual drive subcompact that was nearly flattened by a logging truck outside Watson Lake. In Fairbanks he pursued an M.F.A. in Creative Writing. Like many graduate students in Fairbanks, for a number of years he lived in a "dry" cabin outside of town—one without running water or indoor plumbing—using an outhouse all the winter.

He met his wife, Gerri, in the program and after graduating the two applied to teach English abroad. He and Gerri may have had enough of snow and cold as they accepted positions at a university in Thailand. They lived in Bangkok for four years, Ian taking one year to teach in Japan. While living in S.E. Asia, the two explored Laos, Cambodia, Malaysia, Indonesia, Sri Lanka, and India.

In 1998 they enrolled in a Ph.D. program in English literature. During this time Steven Erikson's Malaz novels found success and Ian was confronted by a difficult decision: seize the moment to pursue his own fantasy writing in he and Steve's co-created world, or continue pursuing his doctoral research.

He chose the former because, while he still regards his research topic as valuable and exciting (in brief: desertion and the myth of "going native" in Nineteenth Century fiction and nonfiction of the south Pacific), he feels that what he and Steven have created is something unique: it's a story that would not be told by anyone else and writing it is an extraordinary privilege. Learn more about his and Steven's world of Malaz at www.malazanempire.com.

Cecelia Holland

Cecelia Holland writes historical fiction, because history seems an endless fund of material. She likes novels, because they are long and wide and deep. Every once in a great while, she tries to write a poem, and, now and then, a short story, but she prefer novels. When Cecelia was in college, she took a creative writing course, mostly to get a sure A. Since then, she has written a lot, read a lot, and raised her three wonderful daughters. She lives in the wild country of northern California. Once a week, Cecelia teach creative writing at Pelican Bay state Prison, two hours away in Crescent City, and, every day, she takes care of a small menagerie of little animals. Visit her website at www.thefiredrake.com. Cecelia is pictured above with her grandson Finnegan.

Contributors

Howard Andrew Jones

Howard Andrew Jones can usually be found hunched over his laptop or notebook, mumbling about flashing swords and doom-haunted towers. He has worked variously as a TV cameraman, a book editor, a recycling consultant, and a college writing instructor. He was instrumental in the rebirth of interest in Harold Lamb's historical fiction, and has assembled and edited eight collections of Lamb's work for the University of Nebraska Press. Prior to their first novel length adventure, *The Desert of Souls*, his characters Dabir and Asim appeared in short stories in a variety of publications, and most of those adventures have been compiled in the short story collection *The Waters of Eternity*. He blogs regularly at the Black Gate site www.blackgate.com and maintains a web outpost of his own at www.howardandrewjones.com.

Paul Kearney

The Monarchies of God:
Hawkwood's Voyage (1995)
The Heretic Kings (1996)
The Iron Wars (1999)
The Second Empire (2000)
Ships from the West (2002)

The Sea Beggars:
The Mark of Ran (2004)
This Forsaken Earth (2006)

The Macht:
The Ten Thousand (2008)
Corvus (2010)
Kings of Morning (2012)

Paul Kearney is a Northern Irish fantasy author. He is noted for his work in the epic fantasy subgenre and his work has been compared to that of David Gemmell. He was born in Ballymena, Northern Ireland, in 1967 and studied Anglo-Saxon, Middle English, and Old Norse at Oxford University before spending several years in both the U.S. and Denmark, finally returning to Northern Ireland. He currently lives and writes in County Down in a cottage by the sea, with his wife, three dogs, a beat-up old boat, and far too many books.

Ari Marmell

Ari Marmell would love to tell you all about the various esoteric jobs he held and the wacky adventures he had on the way to becoming an author, since that's what other authors seem to do in these sections. Unfortunately, he doesn't actually have any, as the most exciting thing about his professional life, besides his novel writing, is the work he's done for *Dungeons & Dragons* and other role-playing games. His published fiction consists of both fully original works and licensed/tie-in properties—including *Darksiders* and *Magic: the Gathering*—for publishers such as Del Rey, Pyr Books, and Wizards of the Coast. Ari currently lives in an apartment that's almost as cluttered as his subconscious, which he shares (the apartment, not the subconscious, though sometimes it seems like it) with George—his wife—and two cats who really need some form of volume control installed. You can find Ari online at www.mouseferatu.com.

Janet & Chris Morris

Janet Morris has published more than 20 novels since 1976, many co-authored with her husband Chris. Her first novel, written as Janet E. Morris, was *High Couch of Silistra*, the first in a quartet of novels with a very strong female protagonist. She has contributed short fiction to the shared universe fantasy series *Thieves World*, in which she created the Sacred Band of Stepsons, a mythical unit of ancient fighters modeled on the Sacred Band of Thebes. She created, orchestrated, and edited the Bangsian fantasy series *Heroes in Hell*, writing stories for the series as well as co-writing the related novel, *The Little Helliad*. Janet has also written, contributed to, or edited several book-length works of nonfiction, as well as papers and articles, including the original concept for the U.S. nonlethal weapons program and other papers and articles on developmental military technology and diverse defense and national security topics.

Selected
Merovingen Nights:
Fever Season (1987)
Troubled Waters
(1988)
Divine Right (1989)

~ Co-authored or
edited with Janet
Morris ~

Selected nonfiction:
The American
Warrior (1992)
Weapons of Mass
Protection (1995)

Selected Heroes in
Hell Series (editors):
Lawyers in Hell (2011)
Rogues in Hell (2012)

The Sacred Band of
Stepsons series:
City at the Edge of
Time (1988)
Tempus Unbound (1989)
Storm Seed (1990)
The Sacred Band (2010)
Tempus with his right-
side companion Niko
(2011)
The Fish the Fighters
and the Song-girl
(2012)

Chris Morris began writing music in 1966, fiction in 1984, and nonfiction in 1989. Much of his fiction and nonfiction literary work, including all of his book-length science fiction and fantasy, has been written in collaboration with his wife Janet, with whom he has also written two novels under the joint pseudonym of Daniel Stryker and one novel under the pseudonym of Casey Prescott. He has contributed short fiction to the shared universe series *Thieves' World*, *Heroes in Hell*, and *Merovingen Nights*. He and Janet have also coauthored six titles in *The Sacred Band of Stepsons* series. In the realm of nonfiction writing, Chris has authored books and articles on military and defense matters in collaboration with Janet and others.

Cat Rambo

Collections:
Eyes like Sky and Coal and Moonlight (2009)
Near + Far (2012)

Cat Rambo lives and writes in the Pacific Northwest. Her collection, *Eyes like Sky and Coal and Moonlight*, was a 2010 Endeavor Award finalist. Explore more of Cat's writings at www.kittywumpus.net.

Brandon Sanderson

Mistborn:
The Final Empire (2006)
The Well of Ascension (2007)
The Hero of Ages (2008)
The Alloy of Law (2011)

Alcatraz:
Alcatraz Versus the Evil
Librarians (2007)
Alcatraz Versus the Scrivener's
Bones (2008)
Alcatraz Versus the Knights of
Crystallia (2009)
Alcatraz Versus the Shattered
Lens (2010)

Select novels:
Elantris (2005)
Warbreaker (2009)

The Stormlight Archive:
The Way of Kings (2010)

Robert Jordan's Wheel of Time:
The Gathering Storm (2009)
Towers of Midnight (2010)
A Memory of Light (2013)

Brandon Sanderson grew up in Lincoln, Nebraska. He writes Epic Fantasy, loves mac and cheese, and lives in Utah with his wife and kids. Check out Brandon's online presence at www.brandonsanderson.com.

Jason M Waltz

Anthologies edited:
Return of the Sword (2008)
Rage of the Behemoth (2009)
Demons: A Clash of Steel (2010)

Jason M Waltz still lives in the state he grew up in, after a brief interlude out West—where his heart really lies among the silent deserts and mountains with the lone warriors of blade and bullet. He is an ardent fan of heroic tales and founded Rogue Blades Entertainment with the goal of delivering action adventure with an *Extreme Edge*. One of his greatest desires is that people rediscover the honorable code of heroics through reading his titles, and become inspired to reach beyond themselves and grab that sword in the stone before them.

C. L. Werner

Brunner the Bounty Hunter:
Blood Money (2003)
Blood and Steel (2003)
Blood of the Dragon (2004)

Thanquol and Boneripper Trilogy:
Grey Seer (2009)
Temple of the Serpent (2010)
Thanquol's Doom (2011)

Chaos Powers:
Palace of the Plague Lord (2007)
Blood for the Blood God (2008)

Mathias Thulmann, Witch Hunter:
Witch Hunter (2004)
Witch Finder (2005)
Witch Killer (2006)

The Black Plague:
Dead Winter (2012)

Select novels:
Vermintide (as Bruno Lee) (2006)
Forged by Chaos (2009)
Wulfrik (2010)
The Hour of Shadows (2011)
The Red Duke (2011)
Siege of Castellax (2012)

C.L. Werner holed up in the desert wastes of Arizona, where he pens his poisonous prose with the fang of a ten-button rattler and the gizzard of a Gila monster. In addition to his work for the Black Library, his short fiction has appeared in Rogue Blades anthologies, Cthulhu Codex, Midnight Shambler, and *Inferno!* magazine. He is currently head background writer for *AE-WWII*, the Darkson Designs' tabletop war game of alternate history and supernatural evil. Visit him anytime at www.vermintime.com.

CPSIA information can be obtained at www.ICGtesting.com
Printed in the USA
BVOW07s1552161213

339281BV00001B/118/P